AMBUSHED!

Longarm saw the movement of their gunbarrels and ducked down the alley, legging it hard. Two shots whined off the adobe building's walls, and then came the sudden pounding of their horses as the two men galloped into the alley after him. Longarm ducked into the alley running behind the saloon and flattened himself against the wall.

Both riders charged at Longarm, their six-guns blazing. Keeping low, Longarm stood his ground for a moment and returned their fire, then turned and raced down the alley.

Still running flat out, Longarm fired back over his shoulder at the horse and rider closing on him. The pounding of hooves increased their thunder. Longarm dove to one side. He was not fast enough. . . .

Also in the LONGARM series from Jove

TABOR EVANS

LONGARM

AND THE LOST MINE

JOVE BOOKS, NEW YORK

LONGARM AND THE LOST MINE

A Jove Book/published by arrangement with the author

PRINTING HISTORY
Jove edition/October 1990

ISBN: 0-515-10426-4

Jove Books are published by The Berkley Publishing Group,
200 Madison Avenue, New York, New York 10016.
The name ''Jove'' and the ''J'' logo
are trademarks belonging to Jove Publications, Inc.

PRINTED IN THE UNITED STATES OF AMERICA

10 9 8 7 6 5 4 3 2 1

LONGARM

AND THE
LOST MINE

Chapter 1

The night was still young when Longarm fled the smoky back room at the Windsor Hotel where he had failed for the second time in an hour to fill an inside straight. Leaving the hotel, he dodged a hack pulling up in front and started across the broad avenue, doing his best to dodge the horse buns that lay everywhere in his path. He was not always successful, and each time his mistake caused a familiar and noxious effluvium to greet his nostrils.

Gaining the sidewalk, he headed down Colfax, intent on reaching a familiar address where a widow lady he had known for a while now had promised him brandy and a warm bed for the night. Indeed, he was wondering if it were not this promise that had clouded his judgment during the poker game. A big man, better than six feet tall, he moved along with a smooth, catlike stride, a looming presence that caused those he passed to give way before him without hesitation.

Eager to reach the widow lady's address, he cut down an alley that would take him through the block and out onto the street where the widow lived. Something alerted him; he glanced back and caught sight of a shadowy figure darting into the alley behind him, two more following. There was something furtive in the way they moved, and after Billy Vail's warning earlier that day, he was not entirely taken by surprise.

Dammit, he told himself. *It sure as hell didn't take them long to get here!*

He kept going, and when he reached a point halfway down the alley, pulled up suddenly and glanced back again. The three dark figures hastily ducked into the shadows close alongside the buildings fronting the alley and froze, waiting for him to start up again. There was no longer any doubt about it. These were the three Billy had warned him about, the convicts who had just eloped from Leavenworth, led by his old friend Jason Tanner.

Longarm started up again, keeping his pace steady as he waited for the three to get closer. When he heard the sudden pounding of their feet as they started to run after him, secure in the belief they had him all to themselves in the bowels of this alley, he unholstered his .44-40 from his cross-draw rig and ducked into a doorway. The running footsteps pounded closer. He leaned back against the door. Without warning, the lock gave way and he was catapulted backward into a dank stairwell.

A shout came from the alley. "He's in there! After him!"

Longarm turned and bolted up the stairs, taking three at a time. He burst through a door at the head of the stairs and found himself in a small office. Before him stood a metal filing cabinet, a desk beside it. To the right was a window. Striding over to it, he flung up the sash and peered down into the alley. A shot came from the darkness beneath him and the windowpane above his head shattered. Punching a quick return shot at the gun flash, he heard a man cry out and the sound of his gun clattering to the alley floor. Another gunshot, this one from farther down the alley, smashed what was left of the windowpane. Two more quick shots followed, one of the slugs ricocheting off the file cabinet like an angry hornet.

Hearing the pounding of booted feet on the stairs, Longarm left the window and ducked back out of the office onto the stair landing. A shadowy figure was pounding up the steps toward him. Longarm pumped two quick shots into him. The man cried out, flung up his arms, and went toppling backward down the steps. Charging down after him, Longarm leaped over his crumpled figure and ran back out into the alley.

About twenty yards in front of him, a dark figure pulled up quickly, sent a hurried round at Longarm, then turned and fled back down the alley. Longarm ran after him, but was not able to overtake him before the man reached the gaslit street. For just a moment the man paused to glance back at Longarm, the lines of his face standing out clearly in the steady flame of the street lamp just above him.

It was Jason Tanner, all right.

And then he was gone.

By the time Longarm reached the head of the alley himself, he had to fight his way through a growing, excited crowd drawn to investigate the rattle of gunfire that had filled the alley. Before he could break through the crush and take after Tanner, Longarm found his arms suddenly pinned to his sides as two overzealous town constables grabbed him and slammed him roughly back against a plate-glass window. In their excitement, they nearly broke his wrist as they wrested Longarm's revolver from him. Before he could explain who he was and what he was doing with a drawn revolver in the middle of Denver, someone discovered one of the bodies in the alley, and for the next few minutes Longarm was too busy establishing his identity to continue after Jason Tanner.

When he finally did arrive at the widow lady's apartment about an hour later, she greeted him rather icily. "I'm glad you could make it."

"So am I, Marie," he told her solemnly, doffing his snuff-brown Stetson and entering.

"I was about ready to give up on you." She took his hat from him and hung it on the hat tree, then led him into the living room. She was trying very hard to be cross with him, but he could see it was giving her difficulty.

He held up, then pulled her toward him. "I met an old friend on the way."

"Did you now? Male or female?"

4

"Male."

"You men, you do so love to run in packs."

"But I'm here now."

"Ah, yes," she said, leaning into him, her voice husky, "so you are."

He knew he was forgiven then and kissed her on the lips. He hoped that Jason Tanner hadn't had enough gumption to hold up once he gained the street and keep Longarm in sight, then follow him to this apartment.

Marie's arms tightened about his neck, her moist lips opened, and he decided he would worry about Jason Tanner later.

Vail leaned back in his swivel chair and shook his head. A first-rate lawman in his day, Vail had traded a saddle for the swivel chair and the great outdoors for a desk, and as a result was putting on tallow and losing his hair, a constant reminder to Longarm that he had better stay on his horse chasing owlhoots or the same thing would happen to him.

"Well, now, that sure as hell makes the cheese more binding," Vail remarked. "I figured Tanner might stop by to tend to you—but not so quick. He sure as hell didn't waste much time."

"Those were my thoughts exactly," Longarm told Vail.

"What I don't understand, Longarm, is why you went into that alley after what I told you."

"It was late and I wanted to get where I was going."

"There's a woman in this. I can tell."

"Maybe so, but look at it this way, Billy. Now

5

there's two dead escaped convicts we don't have to worry about anymore."

"I admit, that's some comfort. But Jason Tanner's the one who worries me the most."

Longarm nodded. Tanner was a homicidal maniac, a bank robber who liked to take hostages, then leave pieces of them on the trail for his pursuers to find. One of the hostages he had used in this fashion had been a federal marshal, an old friend of Billy's and a man Longarm had come to know pretty well himself. Two years before, gazing down at what Tanner had left of Billy's old friend, Longarm had vowed to bring Tanner in, and after tracking him almost a month, he *had* brought him in and testified at his trial. But instead of getting the hanging he so richly deserved, Tanner had been given a life sentence, the mealymouthed judge who presided announcing grandly that he did not believe in capital punishment.

And now Tanner—a man who definitely *did* believe in capital punishment—had broken out and the night before had tried to even the score with the deputy U.S. marshal who had brought him in.

"You going to send me after the bastard?" Longarm asked.

"What do you think?"

"You said something about gold stashed in some mine."

"Yeah. Somewhere in Arizona. All I know is what's in that file. One of the two men who broke out with Tanner—his name was Jacob Werner; he's the one you caught on the stairs last night— was always insisting he had a map that would take

6

him to a mine containing sacks of gold he and a fellow prospector had stashed away. Looks like Tanner and another one took the bait and broke out with him so they could get rich and live happily ever after."

"You think maybe that's all it was? A wild story to hook Tanner so he would take the man with him on a break?"

"Might be. It's possible. And then again, maybe there is gold stashed in a mine somewhere in Arizona."

"Which means Tanner will be heading for Arizona, then."

"That's what I figured—less'n he's still hanging around Denver, hoping for a second shot at you."

"I don't think so, Chief—not with two of his buddies dead. I figure he's maybe already pulled out."

"My thinkin' exactly."

Vail lifted a file out of the clutter on his desk and shoved it toward Longarm. "Read what's in there. I just got it from Leavenworth. It'll give you more to go on."

Longarm took the file off Vail's desk and stood up. "I'll go over it this afternoon. Get my travel vouchers ready. I'll take the train first thing in the morning."

"Suits me," Vail said.

"And this time, Billy, I don't think I'll be bringing the son of a bitch back alive."

"I didn't hear that," Vail drawled. Then he smiled. "But you'd be a fool to give that judge another chance to save Tanner's neck."

The file in his hand, Longarm left Vail's office.

• • •

Smiling for the first time in a long time, Long-arm peered across the blistering, sun-blasted wasteland at the entrance to the arroyo below him. He had just glimpsed Tanner approaching it. But only for an instant were the horse and rider visible, and now all Longarm could see was a sheer rock wall and the parched brush shimmering in the heat. He took up his reins and let the big roan pick its way down the slope.

The late afternoon sun rested on his shoulders like a heavy hand. Less than two days behind Tanner when he left Round Rock a week before, Longarm had closed the gap some, but Tanner had managed to keep himself just beyond the next butte or canyon. During this time all Longarm had seen move—aside from himself and his horse—were the few scorpions and lizards darting for shade ahead of his mount's hooves, while above him a patient trio of buzzards drifted in the hot thermals. He was now traveling through a forbidding badlands of towering buttes, narrow, twisting canyons, and arroyos—a dry, waterless land that Longarm was convinced God must have built for practice before he set to work fashioning hell.

A few hours before, Longarm had caught sight of Tanner on the horizon ahead of him, the image of horse and rider shimmering in the terrific heat. Though Tanner had remained visible for only a moment, the sighting had given solidity at last to the hoofprints and dead camp fires Longarm had been coming on. And now, just a few minutes before, Longarm had seen Tanner riding into the arroyo he was now approaching. He was pretty certain Tanner had caught sight of him, and that he was, in fact, drawing him into the arroyo to bushwhack him. As he neared the arroyo's entrance, he lifted his Winchester from its scabbard, and slowed cautiously.

That was when he saw the girl standing on a butte off to his right.

Peering up at her through the hammering heat, he saw her hair was Indian black, and she was wearing a dress so torn there was little left of it. When she saw him looking up at her, she waved, frantically, desperately. He dropped his Winchester back into its scabbard and raised his hand to wave back. At that instant, a man came out from behind a shoulder of rock behind her and dragged her out of sight. Longarm dropped his hand back to his Winchester and frowned. Could that have been Tanner? At this distance he could not be certain; if so, who in hell was the girl?

Turning his horse away from the arroyo, Longarm urged it toward the butte. Before long, he came to its base and saw ahead of him a narrow game trail that looked as if it might take him to the top.

Just inside the arroyo, Tanner watched Longarm turn his horse and gallop away from the arroyo entrance. In a moment he was out of sight. Where in the hell was the big son of a bitch going? Tanner knew the lawman had seen him entering the arroyo. He had made sure of that. So why hadn't he followed him into the arroyo? He swore bitterly. His one good chance to bushwhack the bastard was gone, and he would not soon get another.

Tanner had crowded himself into a narrow cleft between a boulder and the canyon wall. About twenty yards farther on into the arroyo, the dull shine of his horse's carcass lay baking in the sun where it had collapsed alongside the dry streambed. Tanner had not only missed his chance at getting rid of the lawman, he had missed his chance to take Longarm's mount. Now he was afoot.

Dammit, what could have turned the bastard?

Through slitted eyes, Tanner peered out of the arroyo, hoping against hope to see Longarm return. Just before he had turned off the trail, the lawman had glanced up to his right and had started to wave. Who the hell could he have been waving to out here in the middle of this godforsaken wasteland?

Tanner closed his eyes and pushed himself deeper into the boulder's cool shadow. He had to keep his wits about him, he realized—and that meant cool off some, move out, and find out what Longarm was up to. But not now, he told himself dimly. Later, when the sun went down, and it got a little cooler.

He heard his Colt clatter to the ground beside him as he dropped off into an exhausted sleep.

The girl's name was Opal. There was more Apache blood in her than Spanish. But it was the Spanish blood that gave her the tall, willowy figure and the startlingly blue eyes. The rest of her—

including her capacity and willingness to fight—was Apache.

As Glen Harlow dragged her back down the trail, she kicked at him again, this time catching him a nasty crack in the shins. As he bent to his cracked shin, she raked a hooked claw of a hand down his face. Furious, he brought up his six-gun and cracked her on the side of the head. She went sprawling backward, coming down hard on the rocky trail.

When she made no effort to get up, he figured the blow had knocked her out and bent to sling her over his shoulder. She came awake on the instant, striking up at him like a rattlesnake. Her knee found his groin as her fists and elbows punished him about the face and head. Groaning, Harlow backed up, aware that he had a loose wildcat on his hands. He needed help if he was going to bring her back to the mine in one piece.

"Slade!" he cried. "Slade!"

Continuing to pummel him furiously, she tried to snatch the gun from his hand. He pulled his gun back. She sank her bright white teeth into the skin just above his knuckles. With a howl he dropped the weapon. Pouncing on the Colt, she raised it to fire just as a long shadow fell over her. She turned just as Slade brought the barrel of his own Colt down with terrible force onto the top of her head. This time when she struck the ground, she was truly unconscious.

"Give me a hand with her," Slade told Harlow, the trace of a chuckle in his voice as he handed Harlow's gun back to him. "I would have given you a hand sooner, but I liked the way this wildcat

11

came after you. Can you imagine what it's going to be like when we take our turns on her?"

Harlow was a chunky man, little more than five feet five inches tall, with short, yellowish hair and a round, freckled face burnt raw by the Arizona sun. His companion, Slade, was a gray, balding fellow all knees and elbows—a scarecrow of a man with broken yellow teeth.

Harlow looked uncertainly down at the sprawled woman. "Jesus, I don't know about that, Slade. She's some wildcat. Liable to cripple us both, I'm thinkin'."

"Take it from me," Slade assured him, flashing his broken teeth at Harlow. "Once she realizes she ain't got no choice, she'll just lean back and enjoy it. It's in her Indian blood. None of them can resist a white man."

"Yeah? Well, she's sure been doin' all right so far."

Bending, Harlow took the girl's shoulders while Slade grabbed her feet. Together they worked their way back down into a long canyon that ran roughly parallel to the arroyo Longarm had been heading for when he caught sight of the girl. Harlow slung the girl over his shoulder and the two men set off down the boulder-strewn canyon. Off it ran a tangle of steep-sided draws and arroyos, a nightmarish jumble of rock and trails on all sides of them. Indeed, this particular stretch of the badlands, honeycombed with awesome cliffs, box canyons, and twisting gorges—a pitiless nightmare of sun and rock—was one into which countless explorers and prospectors had disappeared completely over the years, never to be seen or heard of again.

They took turns carrying the girl until at last, black ribbons of sweat streaming down both their faces, they reached the mine's entrance and dumped the girl to the ground in front of it. Slade tied her wrists behind her, then bound her ankles. He was not careful as he worked, and Harlow saw how the rawhide cut into the girl's sleek, olive flesh.

"You're cuttin' her," Harlow told his partner.

"I know that," Slade said. "She's goin' to be damn anxious for us to untie her when she wakes up." Slade smiled unpleasantly up at his chunky partner. "And when she does, maybe she'll see her way clear to making a deal with us."

Opal opened her blue eyes. They blazed in fury up at Slade. "Never!" she hissed. "Never will I make deal with the likes of you!"

Before Slade could jump back, she spat up at him, catching him in the face. He wiped it, his fanged mouth twisting into a snarl. "We'll see about that!" He slapped her hard.

"You'll see about what?" a voice demanded from the darkened mine shaft behind them.

Harlow turned as Sam Dillon stepped out into the sunlight.

"This here bitch. She ran off."

"I was wonderin' where the hell you two had gone."

Dillon walked past Slade and looked down at the girl. "You're a real scorpion, ain't you."

The girl did not reply.

Behind them an old-timer emerged from the

mine shaft. His old eyes were dim, his beard was stained mahogany with tobacco juice, and he walked with an arthritic stoop. When he tried to get past the three men to see to the girl, Dillon grabbed him and flung him brutally to one side. He struck the ground with a painful gasp.

"Any luck, Sam?" Slade asked.

"Nothing," said Sam. "Not a goddamn thing."

"Jesus," said Harlow wearily, "and we been here better than a week now."

Somewhere between thirty and fifty, Sam Dillon was a gaunt, filthy man with long, matted hair that ran down past his shoulders. He was the most desperate in appearance of any of them, with a face that would frighten a rebellious child into sainthood. Its right side had been caved in years before by the plunging hoof of a runaway draft horse. Sam had no right cheekbone, and where his eye should have been there was only a filthy, ragged black patch. He took a perverse pleasure in thrusting this broken visage close to the squeamish—especially those women he purchased for a night's entertainment—enjoying the look on their faces as they turned their heads or averted their eyes. Then would he reach out and snap their faces brutally back around, lift off his eye patch, and force them to gaze into that gleaming, puckered eye socket where once an eye had lived.

Sam looked coldly at him. "I'm gettin' riled," he said.

Harlow swallowed. "Why's that, Sam?"

"I'm beginnin' to think this old son of a bitch

is lying. He don't know where the gold is in there any more than the rest of us do."

"That mean you want to pull out?" Slade asked.

"I didn't say that."

"Well, maybe we should," said Harlow uneasily.

Sam looked at him contemptuously. "For a man who ain't got shit and who never will have, you're givin' up pretty damn easy."

"You said it yourself, Sam," Harlow pointed out. "We been here two days now and we ain't seen one nugget."

"It ain't because it ain't in there," Dillon said. "This old bastard is holding out on us. He knows where it is in there, but he ain't takin' us to it. He's stalling."

Slade looked over at the old man. He had dragged himself over beside the trussed girl and was sitting beside her, his back resting against a boulder. When he saw the three men peering over at him, he moistened his dry lips unhappily and seemed to cringe slightly. A mean grin on his face, Sam strode over to him and kicked him viciously in the side. The old man groaned and toppled over.

When he righted himself, Sam kicked him again, harder.

"You bastard!" said the girl.

Ignoring her, Sam reached down and pulled the old man to his feet. "You been holdin' out on us, Bilcher," Dillon told him. "You ain't takin' us to the gold. You're hopin' we'll give up and leave it for you."

"No!" gasped Bilcher.

"Prove it!"

"Like I said, Jacob swore it was in there. It's in there, I tell you. Sacks of gold, great big nuggets as big as your fist. But we got to go in deeper."

"You damn well better be telling the truth," said Dillon. "If we don't find it soon, we'll bury you and the girl in a pit of scorpions and leave you out here with only your heads showin'. Like the Apaches."

Dillon flung the old man back to the ground. As the ground slammed into his arthritic body, he cried out softly.

"Leave him alone!" cried the girl.

Sam turned to her. What passed for a smile spread across his face. He hunkered down beside her. "They got you trussed good and proper, I see. Now maybe you'll stay put." He slapped her across the face again, then stood up and turned to the others. "How far did she get this time?"

"Far enough," said Slade.

"I was the one caught her," said Harlow. "She had broken on top of a canyon and was waving to a rider below."

"She was *what*?"

"Wavin' to some rider."

"Did the rider see her?"

"I don't know. I was too busy tryin' to haul her in." Harlow shook his head and glanced down at Opal. "She sure as hell put up a scrap. She near broke my shin."

Slade nodded in confirmation. "Yeah. When I came on them, she was getting ready to cut Glen down with his own gun."

Sam grinned at Harlow, shaking his head. "You better watch out, Glen. She'll eat you alive, she will—and then spit you out to make room for dessert." Then he frowned and glanced back down the canyon. "I don't like it. If that rider saw her, he just might come looking for her." He glanced down at the girl. "She would draw a man, at that."

"So what do we do?" asked Harlow.

"Truss up Bilcher, then go take a look. I don't aim to share this gold with anyone."

"If there *is* any gold," said Slade.

"No sense arguin' that now. Tie up Bilcher, I say. Then we'll go make sure that rider ain't comin' after her."

Without further argument, Slade tied up the old prospector as securely as Opal; then the three men set off down the canyon, retracing the route Opal had taken.

Longarm was beginning to feel a little foolish. Now that he had reached the top of the butte, he found it impossible to pinpoint where he had seen the girl grabbed and pulled out of sight. Though at first he had been almost certain that the man who had grabbed the girl was Jason Tanner, he was no longer so sure.

Still astride his roan, Longarm peered about him. Steep-sided canyon walls dropped away on all sides of the bleak, wind-scoured butte and Longarm found himself surrounded by towering chimneylike rock formations, vaulting peaks, and the intimidating, shrouding brows of overhanging rock ledges. Beside the butte, a wall of rock reached into the sky, upon the rim of which great

17

boulders perched, some a bright red in hue, others rust-colored, a few streaked with gold as the dying sun caught their broad flanks. In the distance he could see needlelike projections of rock, a few of them of black basalt, looking as smooth as glass. And over all of the wind-scoured badlands, despite the lateness of the day, hung the soul-shriveling heat of utter damnation.

Longarm urged his mount forward and circled the top of the butte. At last, weary and discouraged, he dismounted. There were no tracks to follow. Nothing. No sign whatever of the brief struggle he had witnessed from below. Walking across a stretch of smooth caprock, he halted and peered down at the canyon below him. A thin tracery of a stream flowed through it. At once he was reminded of how thirsty he was—and how badly his mount must need water as well. He returned to his horse, mounted up, and kept on until he found a narrow, shale-littered game trail leading to the canyon below. He followed it, no longer thinking of the girl. It was the water he craved. About halfway down, the shale and loose gravel under the roan's feet became so treacherous that he was forced to dismount and lead his horse the rest of the way to the canyon floor.

Reaching the stream, he was careful not to let the roan drink his fill at once. Dipping his bandanna in the water, he patted the horse's nose and mouth with it, squeezing the cloth slightly to let some of the water seep into the roan's mouth. Only when he was sure the horse was ready for the water did he allow the animal to drink his fill. Then he went down on all fours himself and drank out of cupped hands, after which he filled all three of his canteens. At the end of it, as a form of celebration, he filled his Stetson with water and solemnly poured it all out over his head and shoulders.

Jesus, but that felt good.

He led the roan over to the cliffside where there was shade and took the saddle off the horse. Peeling off the sweat-soaked saddle blanket, he spent a few minutes drying off the animal, then grooming it. Out here, in this land of rock, sand, and sky, a man without a horse was doomed for sure.

Spotting a patch of grass farther down on the other side of the stream, he led the horse through the stream to the grass and hobbled it. He had no more grain, so the horse would have to subsist on cured grass for a while. Moving back across the stream, he poked carefully about with his rifle barrel to make sure there were no snakes hidden in the rock wall's clefts—and no scorpions either. Then he opened his soogan and eased himself down onto it, his back to the canyon wall. The hot, soul-blistering day was nearly done, and it was time for him to figure his next move.

By going after that girl, he had lost Tanner—at least for the moment. He cursed mildly. He had been so close to him, he could almost smell the man. He realized that Tanner must have known Longarm was tracking him by this time, which meant Tanner was probably planning something nasty—and might well have doubled back into this canyon to look for him. Either that, or he was long gone.

The day's stupefying heat seemed to have struck

the canyon dumb. If it were not for the stream, it would have been as barren as the moon, with not even a bird song to break the awesome, waiting silence. Longarm stirred wearily, his eyes still burning from the alkali dust and the sun's relentless rays. His weariness was bone deep and he was close to sleep, and for a moment he allowed himself to think it would be safe for him to grab some shut-eye and think about Jason Tanner in the morning when he was fresher.

Then, from above him came the thin, rattling sound of a small avalanche as rock and sand spilled down the steep slope to the floor of the canyon less than ten feet in front of him. Fully alert on the instant, Longarm jumped to his feet, flattened himself against the canyon wall, and levered a round into his Winchester's firing chamber. Then he waited.

He heard nothing more as the tiny avalanche halted after depositing a small mound of sand and gravel about a foot high on the canyon floor. The silence deepened, as did the shadows. Then, across the canyon, the roan lifted its head from the grass and glanced up at the wall over Longarm's head, ears flickering nervously.

Stepping out from the wall, Longarm glanced up and saw a man he didn't recognize clambering down the steep slope, a rifle in his hand. About twenty yards farther down the canyon another one was moving closer toward Longarm, keeping close in to the canyon wall. This one had a Colt in his hand.

Longarm took another step out from the canyon wall so that he was in clear sight of the two men.

"All right," he called to them. "Take it easy now. I got both of you covered. Drop your weapons!"

Instead, the one with the rifle ducked behind an outcropping of rock and fired down at Longarm. As the round exploded at his feet, Longarm sighted quickly and fired back. He heard the man cry out, then saw him slump back against the rock wall as his rifle clattered down the slope. The fellow with the Colt began firing wildly at Longarm. The man's aim was so poor, Longarm felt no anxiety as he remained in full sight, levered swiftly, and raised his rifle a second time.

Too late, he heard the crunch of footsteps behind him. He started to turn. Before he could complete it, the canyon wall seemed to collapse onto his skull. His knees gave way and he sank into oblivion.

Chapter 2

Jason Tanner awoke from a heat-shriveling nightmare, sweat swimming on his body, his lips cracked, his mouth as dry as an old newspaper. He had heard shots coming from beyond the arroyo, somewhere close by in this baked land of twisting arroyos, canyons, and gorges. He waited, holding his head steady, hardly daring to breathe. But there was no more gunfire, and the thought occurred to him that perhaps the shots had only been part of his nightmare. But no. Their echoes still persisted dimly in the rocks around him, and seemed to have had their origin close behind the walls hemming him in.

Glancing across the arroyo, he noticed how far the shadows had crept up the rock walls beyond the wash. It was getting a little cooler too, he noticed. This should have made him feel better, but it didn't as he watched the hunched, waddling buzzards pecking at the remains of his horse's carcass. Filthy birds. He shuddered involuntarily as he saw their beaks ripping out long, bloody tendrils of flesh. Beyond them, deeper into the arroyo, there was nothing, only sheer walls of rock.

That son of a bitch Longarm was around somewhere, waiting for him to show. He was sure of it. That gunfire proved it. Maybe he had been shooting at a rattler, or even a rabbit. He picked up his Colt and moved closer to the arroyo wall, bracing his back against it. In doing so, he placed his hand momentarily down on the flat surface of a rock. The rock moved and he yanked his hand away, feeling something hanging onto the back of it. He looked down. A scorpion was clinging to it, its wicked tail coiled over its back ready to sting.

For an instant Tanner froze. Then, with a shriek, he jumped up, waving his hand wildly in an effort to dislodge the scorpion. It broke loose and he felt it pass close by his shoulder, heard it bounce off the wall behind him, then strike his back. He flung himself about and started beating at his clothes. In his panic he let his foot push aside a boulder resting against the wall, and a rattler appeared from a nest under the wall and begun to coil, its head lifting, its dry rattle filling the air with its warning.

Tanner bolted away from the canyon wall and charged across the gravelly streambed. His foot sank into the soft sand beyond it, and he went sprawling, his chin digging a furrow in the hot sand. Opening his eyes and glancing ahead of him, he saw another scorpion, this one only inches from

24

his face. Letting out a soul-shattering cry of terror, Tanner scrambled wildly to his feet and raced off down the canyon. As he passed the horse's carcass, the foul birds feeding on it spread their wings and flapped heavily toward him as they tried to lift into the air. Holding his arms over his head to ward them off, he screamed again and charged wildly off in another direction, his hair standing on end, his mind teetering on the brink.

He was certain now that every obscene, venomous creature in this hellish land was after him personally.

As soon as Slade reached Longarm's unconscious figure, he began to kick him. The slug that had caused him to drop his rifle had only grazed his right arm, but the flesh wound was painful enough, and he was beside himself with fury.

"Hold off there!" Sam cried, yanking Slade back. "We can use this son of a bitch. Look at his size. He can dig for us. I'm sick of digging myself."

Slade stepped back, pressing his bloody bandanna against his wound. "See what the son of a bitch did!"

Harlow came rushing up. "You all right, Slade?"

Slade glanced down at the now-bloody bandanna. "Just a flesh wound. But it's sure bleedin' some."

"We'll let Opal take care of it," Sam said. "I hear tell that's one thing an Injun can do—take care of wounds."

"Yeah," said Slade, his eyes gleaming. "And

then maybe she can take care of something else too."

Sam Dillon looked back down at the sprawled body. "All right," he said. "We'll use him to dig for us—and when we find that gold, he can be the one to load up our pack horses. When we're finished, I'll let you be the one to finish him, Slade."

Pleased, Slade nodded. "Don't worry. I won't have no trouble doin' that."

Hunkering down beside Longarm, Dillon rolled him over onto his back and fished through his pockets. He found a wallet, opened it, swore softly when he saw the badge, took out all the folding money, and placed the wallet back in the man's coat. Taking hold of the gold chain, he yanked the watch out of its vest pocket; the derringer clipped to the other end of the chain came with it. Dillon stood up, letting the watch and the derringer swing in front of Slade's and Harlow's astonished gaze.

"A lawman," Dillon said. "Deputy U.S. marshal. And ain't this here a right fancy belly gun?"

Then he reached down for the lawman's snuff-brown Stetson. It had fallen to the ground a few feet away. Dillon put it on, adjusted it, then looked at the others for their approval.

"Well?"

"It fits, Sam."

Dillon looked down at the big, powerful figure sprawled on the ground at his feet. It was obvious the lawman's frock coat and pants, as well as his boots, would be way too large for him. So he'd let the poor fool keep them while he dug in that goddamn hole for them.

A terrified scream caused Dillon to spin around. The canyon was filled with lengthening shadows by this time and the scream, coming from someone close by, caused all three men to freeze in their tracks. A few moments later there came another scream, a wail of such awful terror that it caused the hair to stand up on the back of Dillon's neck.

"My God," whispered Harlow, the little man edging closer to Slade. "Who the hell is that, Slade?"

"Beats the shit out of me."

"You think it might be an Apache?" Harlow asked Sam. "Torturin' a prisoner?"

"Hell, we ain't seen any Apaches around here."

"That's just it," Harlow reminded him. "You don't never see an Apache—not until it's too late, you don't."

"Hold up, for Christ's sake," Dillon told him angrily. "This here ain't Apache country."

"Opal's got Apache blood."

"That don't change what I just said."

That silenced Harlow and the three stood there, waiting for more screams. When none came and the last echo had faded completely, Dillon turned to Harlow and pointed to the horse the lawman had hobbled on the far side of the stream.

"Go get that horse. We'll sling the son of a bitch over it—less'n you two want to carry him."

Harlow turned and splashed across the stream.

Longarm stirred painfully. It was morning and Harlow, the small, chunky one, was poking him in the ribs with his rifle barrel. Sitting up, he ground his teeth at the rocking pain that was set

27

loose deep inside his skull. But it was not only his head that protested any movement, it was the aching ribs as well. The evening before, the three men had whiskeyed themselves into a lather and then had amused themselves by working him over pretty thoroughly, the fellow he had wounded slightly in the arm going at him with the most enthusiasm.

Longarm blinked up into the short fellow's round, sunbaked face. "What do you want, Shorty?"

"Name's Harlow. Don't call me Shorty. You ready to go to work?"

"What've you got in mind?"

Harlow grinned. "We got a hole in the side of this here mountain. We want you to make it bigger."

Without answering the man, Longarm looked around. Beside him, his thin back to Longarm, the old-timer they called Bilcher was curled up on a blanket still asleep, snoring. The girl, bound and trussed cruelly, was already awake. She had pushed herself back against a boulder and was watching him closely. The night before he had heard them call her Opal.

When her eyes met Longarm's, she smiled fleetingly. He smiled back.

"Oh, you like Opal, do you?" Harlow asked, smirking.

"Yes, you fat son of a bitch. I do."

Longarm's insolence took some of the starch out of Harlow. He looked around at his two partners for support, or at least an indication of how he should respond. Slade, the one Longarm had wounded, came over, his arm resting in a sling. He glared down at Longarm and with mean, careful deliberation kicked Longarm in the crotch. Grimacing silently, Longarm bent over slightly and bit his lip, waiting for the excruciating pain to fade.

"Bastard," Opal said to Slade.

"Leave him be for now, Slade," the leader of this crew said. This one, Sam Dillon, had half his face gone, making him an extraordinarily ugly man. Strolling over now, he peered down at Longarm and remarked to Slade, "If this here lawman's gonna help us, he's got to be able to stand up and walk."

"Sure, Sam," Slade said grudgingly. "Just wanted to put him in his place is all."

"After last night, he knows that well enough."

Sam Dillon turned and, kneeling beside the girl, untied her, then stood back and pulled her up onto her feet. Then, wrapping one arm around her waist, he drew her close and tried to plant a kiss on her lips. She turned her face away from his. He planted a kiss on her neck anyway. She wriggled out of his grasp and slapped him. He punched her. Once in the face, the second time in the belly. She knifed to the ground, then glared up at him.

"You are one big bastard, Sam Dillon."

He laughed. "Now you done hurt my feelings."

"I'll do worse when I get the chance."

The intense, smoldering hatred in her eyes did not seem to daunt the man in the least. "You'll dig with the old man today," he told her. "That ought to cool you down some." He turned to Harlow. "Get the old bastard up."

29

With the same mean insistence he had used on Longarm, Harlow began poking the old prospector in the ribs with his rifle barrel. "Come on, Bilcher!" he said. "Get up!"

Bilcher groaned pitiably and sat up, his eyes squinting in the bright morning sun.

Dillon turned to the fat one. "Take the marshal here in with you and Bilcher—the girl too. Keep them busy. I'll send Slade in to spell you later."

"I ain't had breakfast yet."

"Soon's Slade makes it, I'll see you get some. Now, get a move on. Maybe today we'll find that cache."

Dillon looked down at the girl and the old man then, his face grim. "Today's the day they give babies away with a half a pound of cheese, you two."

"What d'ya mean by that, Dillon?" the old man asked.

"Today you uncover them sacks of gold or we'll figure you been lyin' to us all along."

"It's in there, I tell you."

"Sure it is. So get it out. Otherwise I'll leave you and the girl in there to rot. Seal up the damn hole with you inside. You follow?"

The old man looked unhappily at the girl, then back up at Dillon and nodded. "I follow."

"Then get in there and dig it out."

Harlow waggled the rifle barrel at the three of them. Longarm got up and walked ahead of the old man and Opal toward the mine entrance. When they reached it, Bilcher lit two lanterns, handed one to Longarm, then led the way into the mine. Behind them, Harlow lit another lamp and followed after them.

The deeper Longarm got, the less he liked what he saw. The timbers shoring up the walls and roofing were rotting. In some places less than half a beam was still solid. Moisture was seeping through the walls in an almost steady stream, and before they had gone far they were wading through ankle-deep water.

After what seemed to Longarm a considerable distance, they came to what appeared to be a solid wall of rock. A wheelbarrow and pickaxes had been dumped in the wet muck in front of it, and Longarm could see where Bilcher and the others had tried to cut through the rock. Bilcher held the lantern while Harlow lit some candles. Then, with only the candles to see by, Longarm, Bilcher, and Opal—under Harlow's close scrutiny—began flailing away at the wall. For at least an hour they labored without any appreciable results; it was clear that no matter how hard they worked, they were not going to get through this rock with picks and shovels.

Pausing, Longarm wiped his brow and moved closer to Bilcher. "We need some dynamite," he said in a low voice to the old man. "We're getting nowhere this way."

"Hell, mister, I know that," the old man replied softly, "but that don't matter none. Just keep on working."

"Why, dammit?"

"I'll tell you why later."

"You better tell me now. You heard what Dillon said. He wants whatever the hell you got hidden behind this wall."

"That's just it. There ain't nothin' behind it."

"What are you two mumbling about?" demanded Harlow, moving a step closer to them. "Get back to work, lawman."

Longarm turned to face him. "We need dynamite."

"Well, you ain't gettin' any. You got a big mouth and a strong back. So close your mouth and put your back into it."

As he spoke, he waggled the big Colt he was holding. It was an older dragoon with a barrel seven and a half inches long, making it as heavy as a sinful heart. It had been in Harlow's hand since he followed them into the mine, and Longarm had an idea that maybe Harlow might be just a little weary of holding it on them all this time. And Harlow still hadn't had his breakfast either.

"I just told you, Shorty," Longarm told him. "No dynamite. No results."

"Don't call me Shorty, dammit!"

Longarm took a step toward Harlow and smiled down at the little man, over whom he towered. Harlow took a slight step back. Longarm kept after him, grinning. "Get me some dynamite and I won't call you Shorty anymore. That's a promise."

"Well, dammit," Harlow said unhappily, "I can't *get* you any dynamite. We don't have none. This here crazy prospector said all we had to do was pick up the sacks of gold. Said they was hid

32

in here behind some rocks. He didn't say nothin' about needin' any dynamite."

Longarm turned to Bilcher. "That right, old man?"

Bilcher cleared his throat and nodded. "Well, that's the way I thought it would be."

Out of the corner of his eye, Longarm saw Harlow move close up beside Longarm to hear what Bilcher said. Longarm swung around and grabbed Harlow's wrist with both hands and twisted violently outward. With a sharp cry, Harlow dropped his weapon. Longarm flung the little man violently back against the mine shaft's wall; then, snatching up the dragoon, he stepped closer to the terrified man and clubbed him hard on the side of his head. With a muffled gasp, Harlow dropped to the floor of the mine shaft, his head lolling to one side. Nudging Harlow to make sure he was out, Longarm turned to Bilcher.

"You want to tell me now what the hell is going on here? Where's all this gold Harlow was expecting? And those two out there. Who the hell are they?"

"There's no gold in here," Bilcher told him simply.

Opal stepped closer. "What this old man say is right, mister."

"Well, that sure as hell don't make much sense."

"But it is true," Opal insisted. "Amos and I, we see these riders following us. We know them, and we know what they want. So we lead them to this old abandoned mine. When we reach here,

33

they no believe us when we tell them there is no gold."

"And the more you insisted, the surer they got the gold was in here."

"Yes," Opal said. "So we confess and say they are right."

Bilcher shook his old head. "You can't never tell dishonest men the truth. It ain't in them to know it."

Longarm frowned at the two. "That's a pretty dangerous game you're playing."

Opal said, "We know. We have stall, and yesterday I break away and go for help. When I see you on horse, I think maybe you help us. But when I see what these men do to you last night, I am very sorry what I do. But now I think I am not so sorry." She smiled at Longarm then, her clean teeth gleaming in the dim mine shaft.

"Well, we're not out of this yet," Longarm pointed out. "There's still two of them out there. Keep behind me and stay back until I settle with them."

Longarm moved back through the mine until he caught sight of the bright pinpoint of light ahead of him, then slowed and, crouching, continued on until he reached a spot just inside the mine entrance. Peering out into the brilliant daylight until his eyes became accustomed to the glare, he looked cautiously out of the mine shaft and caught sight of Slade sitting on the ground. He was slumped crookedly to one side, his back against the canyon wall, his mouth open as he snored. His arm was in a sling and he was not wearing a gunbelt. Dillon was bent over the camp fire, his back to the mine entrance as he reached for the coffee pot.

Longarm stepped out of the mine.

"Straighten up slowly, Dillon," Longarm told him.

The man did as he was told, then turned to face Longarm. "Damn that fool, Harlow. I shoulda known."

"Yes, Dillon, you should've."

The palm of Dillon's right hand hovered inches above the grips on his revolver. The tip of his tongue moistened his lips.

"Go ahead if you want, Dillon."

At once the fellow raised his right hand waist high. "I ain't no fool," he said.

"In that case, drop your gunbelt and kick it over here."

Slowly, deliberately, Dillon unbuckled his gunbelt and let it drop to the ground. Then he kicked it over to Longarm, who bent quickly and took his old .44-40 out of the holster and stuck Harlow's dragoon into his belt. Then he glanced over at Slade.

Fully awake, Slade peered into the bore of Longarm's gun. "How the hell did you get loose?" he wanted to know.

"Never mind that, Slade. Just get up and join Dillon over there."

Slade got to his feet and walked over to stand beside Dillon. Longarm looked toward the mine and called out to Bilcher and Opal, telling them it was safe to come out now.

Then he walked over to Slade and Dillon.

"Both of you sit down cross-legged," he told

them. "And I'll be wanting my watch and derringer, Dillon."

Dillon dug the watch and derringer from a baggy side pocket and handed them to Longarm. As Longarm dropped the watch and derringer back into his vest pockets, Bilcher and Opal emerged from the mine.

"Now we got the bastards," said Opal, her eyes gleaming with excitement. "What're we gonna do with them?"

"I say we kill them," said Bilcher without hesitation. "They beat up on me somethin' fierce."

"I was thinking of herding them into the mine," Longarm said. "It's nice and cool in there. We could truss them good and proper, and by the time they got free and dug their way out, we'd be long gone."

"You are too soft," said Opal. "Amos is right. We should kill these two and be done with it."

"Sorry. I can't do that."

Sam Dillon grinned. "Eat your heart out, bitch. He's a lawman. He can't murder no one. It ain't in the rule book."

"Well, then," Bilcher sighed, "let's get to it then."

He walked toward Slade, and was about ready to order Slade to get up onto his feet when Slade fired up at him through his sling. As Bilcher staggered back, Slade swung the gun out of the sling and aimed at Longarm. Longarm fired twice into Slade's chest. Slade slipped sideways and dropped his gun. Before Dillon could snatch it up, Longarm stepped quickly forward and kicked it away.

"How bad's the old man hurt?" Longarm asked Opal.

She was bent over Bilcher, ripping open his shirtfront to inspect the chest wound. After one quick glance, she looked over at Longarm. "It's bad," she said, her voice trembling with concern. "Real bad."

"Leave him for now," Longarm said, "while we stow this one in the mine shaft."

Longarm herded Dillon ahead of him into the mine, and while Opal bound his wrists and ankles with wet rawhide, he went on further into the mine, aroused the unconscious Harlow, and prodded him ahead of him to where Dillon now lay on his side, trussed like a turkey. Wasting no time, Opal tied Harlow as securely as she had Dillon. Longarm saw the grim satisfaction she took in pulling the rawhide tight.

Back outside, Longarm examined Slade. He had wasted his second bullet. The first one had entered just over Slade's heart, killing him instantly. He walked over then to where they had propped up the old prospector. Opal had not exaggerated. The slug had caught Bilcher in the chest just above his lungs, shattering his collarbone. Where the slug had ranged from there, Longarm could not tell. But there was no exit wound, which meant it was still in his chest, resting in his right lung somewhere.

He left the unconscious man and walked over to where the horses were tethered. They would have to saddle up, move out fast, and get the old man to a doctor who could take out that bullet.

Otherwise, within a few days or less, Bilcher would be a dead man.

Earlier that same morning, Jason Tanner awoke to find that he was alive and that during the night he had not been devoured by wild animals or stung to death by scorpions or rattlers. In this hideous, sun-blasted universe of sky and desert, there was still some mercy, after all.

His wild panic had taken him to a small cave, where he had remained, lapping like a beast at the water seeping through the cracks in the wall. The water had calmed him and he had slept most of the night through. With great patience he managed to fill his canteen from the water oozing out of the rock wall, and with this accomplished, left the cave and returned to the arroyo's entrance, where he had been waiting for Longarm to show the day before. There he picked up his saddlebags, his revolver. Leaving the arroyo, he trudged off, heading in the direction he had seen Longarm take.

It was still cool. The sun had not yet managed to climb above the squat mesas and towering cliffs that loomed on all sides of him. He found the tracks left by Longarm's mount, and was soon at the foot of a game trail that led up onto a butte. Before he could follow it, he heard three shots. The last two sounded like rifle fire. They came from a canyon on the other side of the butte. Circling the butte quickly, he found fresh hoof-prints in the sand and followed them into the canyon.

Splashing into the stream that cut through it,

he ducked his head under for a moment to cool himself off, then splashed on through it. As he reached the other side of the stream and started to move deeper into the canyon, he thought he heard the distant drum of hoofbeats. As he lifted his head to listen, they faded rapidly.

He hurried on down the canyon after the hoofbeats, his heart sinking to think he had come this close to finding help, when he heard faint, muffled shouts, then cries, for help. He kept going, his revolver out now, his eyes searching the rocks above him and the tangle of brush and boulders at the base of the canyon's walls.

The cries remained curiously muffled, as if they were coming from inside a barrel. Or a cave. The cries died away and did not resume. He kept on nevertheless, and rounding a boulder, he saw ahead of him across the floor of the canyon a small grassy sward with two horses grazing on it, and just beyond the horses, the entrance to a mine. A camp fire in front of the mine shaft was still sending blue tendrils of smoke into the air. And beside the camp fire he glimpsed a still body slumped facedown. He couldn't be absolutely sure the man was dead, but the body had that empty look about it—as if all the air had leaked out.

Abruptly, the cries for help—or was it outrage?—erupted again from inside the mine shaft.

Jason's heart had leaped when he saw the horses, plus all the gear scattered about—the bedrolls, saddlebags, and such—and he wasn't all that anxious to share it with whoever was inside the mine doing all that yelling. Still, he was mighty curious about what had gone on here. Maybe it had something to do with Longarm. He crossed the canyon and inspected the sprawled body. There were two bullet holes in the man's chest. He was dead, all right. Skirting the smoldering camp fire, he approached the entrance to the mine and peered into it. But coming so recently from the canyon's brutal glare, he couldn't see anyone.

"Who's that in there?" he demanded.

"Never mind that," an angry voice responded. "Whoever you are, get in here and untie us."

"What happened?"

"Goddammit, never mind that. Get us out of here."

"Sure. Just tell me what happened."

"We got robbed, that's what. Someone came along and stole our horses."

"That's funny. They're still out here. Along with a dead man."

"Damn you, mister. What're you standin' out there for? Come in here and untie us and we'll make it worth your while."

By this time Tanner's eyes had adjusted to the dimness of the mine shaft, and the sunlight behind him cast enough light into the shaft to enable Tanner to see clearly the two men trussed securely about ten yards further in, their backs hard against the shaft wall. His gun trained cautiously on the two men, he moved into the mine shaft and halted a few feet from the two.

Both men had their ankles trussed with rawhide, their hands tied behind them. One of them looked innocuous enough, a small chubby fellow who seemed to have been fashioned from bread dough. At the moment, as he struggled to get his hands free, he seemed on the verge of tears. The other man was a different story entirely. He was the ugliest son of a bitch Tanner had ever seen. His cheekbone had been stove in, and there was an awful hole where his eye should have been. He probably wore a patch over the socket, but it must've fallen off.

This was the fellow who spoke up. "You seen enough, mister? Come closer and cut me loose."

"Maybe you better tell me what this is all about."

"I told you. We was robbed."

"By whom?"

"A lawman."

"A lawman named of Long—Custis Long?"

"That's the son of a bitch, all right."

"You mean he's the one shot that poor bastard out there?"

"Yeah. He's the one. Now untie us."

"Ain't that funny? I'm the one he's after. How come he messed with you guys?"

"You goin' to cut us loose?"

The other one, eager to placate Tanner, spoke up then. "He's lit out with an old prospector and an Apache girl. He ain't actin' like no lawman. He smells gold."

"What's that? Gold, you say?"

"Shut up, Harlow!" the other one told him.

But Harlow was too anxious to ingratiate himself with Tanner. "That's right. The prospector knows where there's sacks of gold dust stashed out here in an old mine shaft."

"You mean this here shaft ain't the place?"

41

"The son of a bitch was holding out. He led us to this mine to stall us."

Tanner looked over at the one-eyed one. "That right?"

With the cat already out of the bag, he nodded sullenly. "That's right," he admitted. "And we fell for it."

"But now you know for sure the gold ain't in here."

"We just figured it out."

"But we got the bastard," said the little fat man. "He's wounded bad. He won't get far."

"That's right," said One Eye. "Cut us loose and we'll go after them with you. If we catch up to the old bastard before he dies, we'll pistol-whip the truth out of him. It's a chance. Throw in with us and you could be a rich man."

But something had already occurred to Tanner. "Hold on. What did you say this prospector's name was?"

"Bilcher."

"*Amos* Bilcher?"

"That's the one. You know him?"

Tanner straightened up. "Well now, ain't that somethin'. You might say I know about him. And he's wounded, wounded bad?"

"He took a slug in his chest."

Tanner swore. "Shit. That's like killin' the goose that lays the golden egg, ain't it?"

"Enough palaver, dammit," said the one-eyed man. "Untie us and we'll go after them. We'll help you get rid of that lawman; then we can all go after the gold."

"You ain't done so good up to now."

"We know better now."

"So do I."

Tanner turned and started from the mine shaft.

"Hey! You gonna leave us here?"

"What do you think?"

"Mister," One Eye warned, "you're making a big mistake!"

Tanner kept on until he reached the mouth of the mine shaft. Then he turned and dropped a pocketknife to the ground. "I ain't all bad," he said. "Here's a knife. Cut yourself loose."

"Dammit! That's no help! We're bound hand and foot!"

"It's the best I can do."

"Damn you! Damn your miserable eyes, mister! I'll find you if I have to ride through the gates of hell to do it!"

"Yep," Tanner said, stepping out into the sunshine. "That's just about what it'll take."

Chapter 3

Bilcher was having a difficult time staying on his horse. Opal was a superb rider, however, and was able to keep her mount close beside the old man's horse as they rode, helping Bilcher to cling to his saddlehorn. The afternoon sun was pitiless, and it soon became obvious to Longarm that Bilcher could not keep on going for much longer. The prospector's saddle was already slick with blood, and though his old hands clasped the horn with desperate strength, his eyes were closed and his head lolled as loosely as a rag doll's. When his black hat finally toppled from his head, Longarm pulled up and dismounted.

"He can't go any further," Longarm told Opal.

Without comment, she slid from her saddle and gave him a hand as he pulled the old man's slack figure from the saddle. Together, they guided the nearly unconscious man over to a shady spot in among some rocks.

Bilcher licked his parched lips. "Water," he murmured. "I'm burnin' up."

Longarm unscrewed his canteen and started to hold it up to Bilcher's mouth, but Opal took it from him, slipped her arm under Bilcher's head, and lifted him so he could drink it. Some color returned to the old man's parchmentlike face and he managed a smile.

"Just leave me here, Opal," he told the girl. "I'm done for and this is as good a place as any."

"We're taking you home."

"No. Too far. Too damn far."

"Then we'll take you to Red Rock. Get the doctor there."

He shook his head wearily. "Too late. Too late. I'm a dead man, I told you."

"No need to talk like that," said Longarm.

"Don't argue with me, mister," the old man rasped angrily, his rheumy eyes suddenly blazing. "I don't want to go no farther. I want to rest. I'm tired. Just let me be."

Opal looked at Longarm, tears coursing down her cheeks. Longarm screwed the cap back on his canteen and stood up, realizing the two wanted to be alone. He walked over to his horse and dropped the canteen's loop over the saddlehorn.

When he looked back at them, they were talking quietly. At last, the old man lifted his hand and held it against the girl's cheek. She took his hand in hers then and kissed it. A moment later he thought he heard her soft gasp of dismay, and saw her bend over and kiss Bilcher's thin forehead, after which she hugged the old man's frail body to her breasts and rocked slowly back and forth, a thin, wailing cry coming from her. Longarm kept his distance and waited patiently, and after a while, she stopped her wailing, let the old man's head rest on the ground, and stood up. Longarm started toward her then. There were no tears, but her eyes were filled with sorrow.

"We must bury him," she said.

Longarm glanced around. This was hard, sun-baked ground—rock mostly. Digging in such ground would not be easy, not without a shovel or a pickax.

She knew at once what he was thinking. "Yes, I know. We cannot bury him here, but I will find a place where no coyotes or wolves will find his body. I promised him that. Stay here by him. I will return soon."

She mounted up and rode off. Longarm found a water hole below the trail and watered his horse, filled his canteens, then took out a cheroot. As he was lighting up, she returned and, dismounting, hunkered down beside him.

"You got a smoke for me?"

He lit a cheroot with his own and gave it to her.

She took it and leaned back, inhaling deeply. "I have found a place."

"That's good."

"But I would like to finish this smoke first."

He nodded.

A few minutes later, they returned to the old man, wrapped him in his slicker, and tied him over his saddle. With Opal in the lead, Longarm mounted up and, leading Bilcher's horse, they set

47

off, heading almost due west until they reached a plateau. Then they let their mounts pick their way carefully down off it into a narrow canyon, and here Opal pulled up.

Longarm and Opal dismounted.

"Over there," Opal said, pointing. "In that cleft."

She was pointing to a ledge at least six feet off the ground and about ten yards into a cleft in the canyon wall.

"There are plenty stones nearby," she said. "We can wedge them in close beside the old one's body and cover him completely. The buzzards will not see him and the coyotes will be unable to reach the ledge."

Longarm nodded. She had chosen well.

"Let's get it done," he said.

Along about nightfall, with the badlands well behind them, they found a patch of scrub oak and willows alongside a narrow stream and made camp. After their supper of hardtack, jerky, and coffee, Longarm slumped down with his back to a log in front of the fire. Opal sat cross-legged beside him and joined him in a smoke.

The firelight caused her long dark hair to take on occasional red highlights. Her luminous eyes appeared fathomless. She had been wearing a loose-fitting skirt and blouse, but Slade and Sam Dillon's ill-usage had reduced one shoulder to tatters; a flap hung down off her bronzed shoulder, revealing a goodly portion of one breast. She appeared unaware of the affect this might have on

Longarm as she sat calmly beside him, puffing on her cheroot.

Abruptly, looking slyly over at Longarm, she reached into her cleft and produced a much-folded parchment—a map, he realized suddenly.

"Before he die, Amos tell me where in his saddlebag he keep this," she told him. "Now it is just the two of us. Amos said it was all right if I tell you about it."

"Maybe you better start from the beginning."

She nodded and began her tale. While working at the Gold Nugget Saloon in Red Rock as a bar girl, she had befriended Bilcher after he came to her aid one night and got the shit kicked out of him in the process. She quit the saloon and went to Bilcher's cabin to look after him; at Bilcher's request, she remained with him from then on as his woman.

"He was no longer fully a man," she told Longarm with a sad smile. "But he was a good man and treated me well. I was like his daughter. But I was sure to make everyone think it was more than that. It was good for people to think this and it made him proud."

Longarm smiled.

About two weeks ago, she went on, Bilcher got a letter from an old buddy of his, and in the letter was the map to a mine where they had cached sacks of gold dust they had stolen from a Wells Fargo shipment, and which Bilcher had tried many times to find again without luck. All he had known for sure was that the mine was in these badlands somewhere. His buddy's map, on the other hand, pinpointed the mine's exact location. It was while

Opal and Amos were following the map that they were overtaken by Sam Dillon and the other two.

"That letter, Opal, the one containing the map. You have any idea where it was mailed from?"

"A prison."

"Leavenworth?"

"I am not sure."

"Was Amos's buddy named Jacob Werner?"

She was amazed. "How you know such a thing?"

"Jacob Werner just broke out of Leavenworth with two others; one of them is still at large. He's the one I was tracking when you waved to me from that butte."

"Jacob Werner is dead?"

"He tried to take me in a back alley in Denver— him, another one who's dead, and a man called Jason Tanner."

"And this Tanner, he is the one you are after now?"

"Yes. There's something else. Tanner's not here by accident. My guess is he was after Amos—and this map here. The way I see it, Jacob Werner sent the map to Amos, to keep the gold out of Tanner's hands. That way, he could be sure Tanner wouldn't kill him after he got it. As long as Amos had the gold, Werner figured he was safe."

"But now he is dead."

"That's right."

"So, and I think maybe we will not let this Tanner get the map either."

"That's right. And it'll make a nice piece of bait."

"To catch this man?"

"Yes."

"You want him bad, hey?"

"I want him very much."

"But what about the gold?"

"That comes second—if at all."

"You are very strange man."

"Not really. I'm a lawman is all."

She finished her smoke, then leaned forward over the map, studying it intently. "I know where this canyon here is," she said, pointing to a line on the map. "The mine is inside it."

"That's nice."

She looked back at him, evidently puzzled that all this talk of gold did not set his pulse to racing. Every man she had ever known had gold fever. Why was this tall lawman different, she was asking herself.

Abruptly, she refolded the map, put it back in her cleft, got up, and moved off into the night. He was thinking of turning in himself when she returned, materializing out of the inky blackness beyond the fire, her naked figure caught suddenly in the blazing firelight. Without a pause, she walked around the fire and came to a halt inches from his upraised face.

Longarm flicked away his cheroot.

"For long time I live with old man who love me but who cannot show it like a man," Opal told Longarm. "Now I want the love of a healthy man who is not a pig like those others. Do you understand, Custis Long?"

"I been thinkin' along them lines myself."

"That is good. I have already made soft bed of willow rushes close to the stream."

She reached down and took his hand. He rose and followed her.

Overhead the silver-dollar moon watched as she dropped lightly to the blanket she had placed over the willow rushes and reclined on her back to wait for him to drop to the blanket beside her. He gazed down, drinking in the sight of her. The moonlight cast a sheen over her body. Smiling up at him, she scissored her thighs apart slightly, and he became aware of her fingers moving in the dark patch between her legs, the sight hitting him like a slug of raw whiskey on an empty stomach. His mouth dry, the blood pounding in his temples, he shucked off his clothes and dropped to the willow bed beside her. He ran his big, callused hand over her thrusting breasts, then down her rounded belly into the curly muff between her thighs.

She sighed and leaned her head back.

He moved up onto her and felt himself probing eagerly against her moist triangle. She raised her thighs to give him entrance and he plunged into her and stayed there, pressing her into the earth. Her breathing came faster, shallower. He withdrew, then plunged in again, much deeper this time, driving himself in as far as he could go, impaling her. Again and again he thrust deep into her. Grunting with pleasure, she flung her arms around his neck and, leaning her head back, lifted herself to meet each thrust.

"Good!" she muttered through clenched teeth. "That is good, Custees!"

Gripping her tiny buttocks with his big hands, he slammed her up into him, feeling her fingers digging into his shoulders, seeing her head snap back and forth now, her lips pulled back against her pearl-white teeth, her face frozen into a sleek, hard grimace.

He slowed then, teasing her, moving back when she wanted him to plunge deeper, breaking the rhythm deliberately, denying her what she wanted. Furious, she snarled at him, then reached up to claw him. He ducked away and she began to whimper as she tried to recapture the rhythm, then rose up onto her elbows.

"Damn you, gringo!" she cried. "Now! Now! I want you now!"

He laughed then and rammed full force deep into her, slamming her to the makeshift couch, driving once more into her, this time with no intention of slowing or pulling back. He caught a glimpse of her jiggling, sweat-pearled breasts, saw her head begin flipping from side to side again, the hard grimace once more returning to her face; and he found he was not capable of holding back any longer as his need surged like a flood within him, driving him on until he felt himself sweeping over; and then they were clinging to each other in a wild, fierce, clawing peak. Crying out, they clung to each other for a long, spasming moment, then relaxed.

He felt her arms falling from around his neck as he fell forward onto her, then rolled off, his hand resting loosely on one of her breasts. With a barely audible sigh, she placed a hand over his, pressed it down upon the breast, and lay there, content. They didn't say a word as they waited for their racing pulses to return to normal.

"*Sí*," she said, turning her head to gaze at him.

"That is what it is like. I remember now."

"That's good."

"You goin' to sleep now?"

"That depends."

She turned to face him and he let the sight of her in the moonlight kindle him once again. He took his hand off her breast and ran it along the soft swell of her breasts, letting her nipples react to the rough drag of his big hands moving across them. When they had become as hard as bullets, he moved his hand back down her body, over the swell of her belly, coming to rest once more in the soft, curly moistness of her pubis. Moaning softly, she lifted her arms above her head and reveled in his caresses, delighting in the feel of his fingers as they moved back and forth along the inside of her thighs. She spread her legs and, through his touch, he could feel the fire building within her.

He glanced down at himself. He was ready again. He eased himself up onto her and then into her. She sighed and let her arms enclose him. What happened then was entirely different from the first time. It was as if the moonlight had fused them into one single, throbbing body, expressing an endless rhythm that was bringing them to climax almost without effort. When at last the pace began to build, it wasn't he who made it build, nor she; it was both of them fused together into a single, rising tide.

Even when they exploded, there was no frantic lunging, no hard breathing, only a series of gasps as together they writhed and clung to each other until the long, sweet pull of it had subsided. Afterward, they lay silently side by side, Opal on her back beside him.

It was Opal who spoke first. "This gold. Is this what you want?"

"No. I want the son of a bitch who tried to kill me in Denver. He's after the gold too, so I'll stick close by you until he shows up. The fact that he got this far tells me he knows the gold is nearby."

She laughed huskily. "Then you will be satisfied with me?"

"Of course."

They were silent a while. Then he said, "We better get back up to the camp fire."

"No. It is safer down here, away from the campsite. Besides, you do not need the fire. I will keep you warm."

As she spoke, she slipped up onto him and then eased back, smiling down at him as he entered her. "You have a great hunger," he commented, leaning back and enjoying it.

"Yes," she agreed softly. "I spend long time with that old man."

Delight followed and built to another delicious climax, after which he sank into a deep, dreamless sleep.

When he awoke the next morning, Opal was gone.

Opal had awakened at dawn and, without disturbing Longarm, had returned to the campsite, dressed, then taken the coffee pot to a spot downstream and filled it. Returning to the campsite, she built up the nearly dead camp fire, then dropped a fistful of coffee into the pot and set it down on the blazing coals. Then she left to check on the horses. They had drifted some distance downstream and she found hers fetlock-deep in the shallows, cropping the soft, sweeter grasses that hugged the embankment. She pulled it out, unbuckled its hobbles, and then peered downstream. Longarm's horse and the spare that had belonged to Amos were not in sight; but since they were hobbled and could not get far, she made no effort to go after them.

She would leave that chore to Longarm when he woke up.

As she turned then to lead her horse up to the campsite, she saw a man she had never seen before standing in her way, his six-gun in his hand, a grin on his face as he leveled it at her.

"Where's the lawman?" he asked.

"I don't know who you mean."

"Sure you do. And where's Bilcher?"

"Dead."

"The old bastard didn't make it, huh?"

"No, he didn't."

"So where's Long? Don't tell me he's dead too?"

She hesitated a moment, then shrugged. "He has gone after a man who tried to kill him in Denver, an escaped convict."

Tanner laughed. "That so? Well, good luck to him."

"Who are you?"

He grinned. "I'm the one he's after. Name's Tanner. Jason Tanner. But you can call me Jason, if you want."

Opal did not like the man. And if Custis was

after him, she knew he must be very dangerous. He was unshaven, his eyes red-rimmed, his lips cracked and broken, and his face tapered to a point, so that his chin was narrow and weak, his teeth protuberant and yellow, like fangs. He resembled an insect someone had stepped on without killing.

"Why should I call you Jason? Why should I call you anything? I will not be with you."

"Sure you will. It's been a long time since I been with a woman."

"I will give you no pleasure, gringo."

"Not at first. I figure you'll have to be worked over some. But you'll come around."

"And that is what you want?" she asked coolly. "A woman you can force?"

He shrugged. "First things first. I just came from the mine where you and Longarm left them two all trussed up. From what they told me you're on your way to the gold."

She was not familiar with this way of addressing Custis Long. *Longarm*. That was maybe a good name for one such as he.

"If you know that," she said, "you know they wound the old man."

"They mentioned it."

"Now he is dead and I do not know where the gold is."

"Sure, you do. I know for a fact Bilcher had a map, and if I'm any judge of human nature, the old fool gave it to you before he died."

"Why you say he have map? How you know such a thing?"

He grinned at her. "He had a map because Jacob Werner sent it to him."

"I don't care what you say. I have no map."

He stepped closer and struck her on the side of the face with his gun barrel. She hit the ground hard, dazed, and before she could react, he had reached boldly into her cleft and pulled out the map. He stepped back and grinned down at her.

"You crazy women," he said, flipping open the map. "You always think nobody will look there— and hell, that's the first place we *do* look."

She got shakily to her feet, seriously considering rushing the man. If his gun discharged in the struggle, it would arouse Custis. But maybe that was not such a fine idea. Custis would come running and this animal would shoot him down in cold blood. No. She would do nothing to endanger Custis. This one she would handle herself. Later. When the time came.

"Those two men in the mine," she said. "Harlow and Sam Dillon. Did you free them?"

He looked up from the map, a confused frown on his face. "Don't worry. By the time they get free, it'll be too late for them to catch up to us."

"You have the map. Leave me and go after the gold. You can have it all for yourself."

"Not likely. I can't read this goddamn map. There ain't even any north and south on it. But I'll bet you can read it. Otherwise, Bilcher wouldn't've given it to you, and you wouldn't've kept it. So it looks like you and me are partners now."

"Never."

He walked closer. "Do you want another crack?

This time I might break your jaw and then you wouldn't be able to eat."

"Or talk. How would I help you then?"

"Yeah," he said, stepping back. "That would make it awkward. All right, come on. We'll go back to your campsite. I can smell the coffee from here."

All the way back up the long trail to the camp, she kept expecting to see Longarm step out from ambush, his gun leveled on Tanner; but they drank the coffee, Tanner stomped out the fire, and she packed her gear and saddled up. Then she rode out with Tanner, and Longarm, still sound asleep alongside the stream at the spot where she had taken him, did not hear a sound.

It reminded her once again how hard and deep a man sleeps after making love.

Chapter 4

Tanner and Opal halted at a water hole at mid-morning. Jumping from his horse, Tanner drank his fill, gulping the water down so fast, he got sick. Watching him contemptuously, Opal took care of her horse before slaking her own thirst, slowly sipping the water from her cupped hands, after which she filled her canteens. The second time Tanner drank more carefully; only then did he see to his mount.

Obviously feeling much better, he approached Opal. She was relaxing in the shade provided by the scrub willows surrounding the water hole. Watching him approach, Opal knew that he wanted her. Badly. He wasn't thinking of gold now. That could wait. But when he caught the withering contempt in her eyes, he pulled up, uncertain.

"Just thought I'd see if you was all right," he told her, grinning suggestively. "I sure wouldn't want nothin' to happen to my pretty little Apache. No, I surely wouldn't."

"Don't come any closer, pig."

"Hell, there ain't no need for you to talk like that. How we gonna be friends, you talking like that?"

"We never be friends."

"Why not? We're partners now."

"I am not your partner. I am your prisoner."

"Sure, if that's the way you want it." He moistened his lips as he looked her over, noting one bare, bronzed shoulder and the long rips in her skirt revealing sleek legs and silken flanks. "But it don't have to be that way."

"Yes, it does."

"Come on," he cajoled. "Ain't no need to be like that. Go easy on me. I'm only human."

"Sure. I go easy on you. I will not kill you while you sleep."

"Well, now. That's more like it."

Her teeth flashed in her dusky face. "I will not kill you because I want others to have that pleasure."

Her words shook him like a fist out of darkness. He could not withstand the awful, implacable loathing he saw in her eyes, the coiled, expectant way she held herself. He could tell that if he took one step closer, she would hurl herself up at him with all the fury of a cornered wildcat, her fingers raking his face, blinding him if possible. She was part Apache, after all. Maybe she was not for him. Not right now anyway.

Turning away, he found another shady spot near the water hole and after inspecting the ground all around him, sat down and made himself a smoke. He could feel her watching him alertly all the while. It made him damned uneasy. He hurriedly finished his smoke, got up, and told her they were moving on.

She didn't argue and mounted up quickly before he got to his own horse, all fresh and ready while he was still as frazzled as ever. Moistening his dry, cracked lips, he could feel her eyes on him as he approached his horse and took up its reins. As he hauled himself wearily into his saddle, he was dimly aware that for now, at least, it was not he who had her, it was she who had him.

This galled him and made him want to strike out at her, cut her up some maybe, and stake her out. He'd like that. Leave her for the buzzards. But he had to keep a hold on himself and play this smart. He needed her, dammit, and he must not allow himself to forget that. Besides, right now he was too drained to do anything. Tonight, maybe. Yeah. He'd fix her good tonight. He knew a way to make a woman beg for it. None of them liked pain, not the kind of pain he knew how to generate. This pleasant thought revived his spirits somewhat, gave him an incentive.

He glanced covertly over at her and caught the faint glimmer of a smile on her face an instant before she booted her horse out in front of him and headed toward the mouth of a canyon in the distance.

"How much farther?" he shouted angrily after her.

"Not be long now," she yelled, without looking back.

Digging his spurs into his horse, he followed after her, riding out into the full blast of the sun, wincing as he felt its awful weight once more, his eyes squinting into the dust she was raising. Under the sun's cruel eye, they rode on for what seemed forever, clattering through canyons, up steep shale-littered grades, across sun-flooded ridges, twisting and turning, moving ever deeper into this blasted wilderness of stone and sand and cacti.

He hated this land. Everything in it had a rattle, a thorn, or a sting.

They were following a streambed. There was no trace of water in it, only gravel and sand and a few dark patches, where once water had stood. Opal had been drawing steadily ahead of him, and he was thinking of calling out to her, but his mouth was dry, his tongue heavy. Maybe if he sent a shot over her head, she'd hold up.

But he did nothing. The sun had smote him into an insensate weariness, robbing him of judgment. Opal led him up the side of a steep draw. The last few feet made for a hard scramble as his horse's hooves slipped on the shifting gravel and shale. He finally dismounted and led the horse—with cruel, angry yanks on the reins—up the steep slope to the crest. When he gained it he found Opal already far ahead of him, lashing her horse as she lifted it to a hard gallop. He mounted up and rode furiously after her, but that only seemed to increase her speed, and he knew at once that she intended to outdistance him, leave him behind in this hellish land.

He clawed his six-gun from its holster and sent three quick rounds after her, each shot apparently as futile as the one before it. He pulled up as his horse lurched unsteadily. His senses reeling from the effort to overtake her, he swore bitterly as he watched her dim, shimmering ghost vanish among the rocks.

"That bitch," he croaked half aloud. "I shoulda killed her when I had the chance."

He slipped from his horse and led it into the shadow of nearby rocks close against the arroyo's steep rock wall. The only thing he had to comfort him now was the knowledge that he had the map—but at that moment, now that he was lost in this hellish landscape, it gave him little comfort.

"You hear that?" cried Dillon, pulling his horse up.

"I heard. Shots, three of them."

"Over there, to the north. Let's go."

Despite the heat, they pushed their horses to the limit, clattering across a sun-bleached flat and plunging into a narrow arroyo. As they galloped along, someone who had taken refuge in the rocks ahead of them stepped into view and waved at them frantically.

The two men pulled to a shuddering halt beside the man, grinning down at him, pleased at this wicked reversal in their fortunes. They could see that only after he had left the rocks had the fellow recognized Dillon's eye patch and ruined face. But by then it was too late.

"Well, well, you son of a bitch," said Dillon, his right palm caressing the butt of his six-gun.

"Looks like I done what I said I would. I followed you all the way into hell."

Beside him on his horse, Harlow chuckled. This he was really enjoying.

"I see you two got loose," the man said, watching them through narrowed eyes, while he edged back carefully toward the rocks.

"That we did. But no thanks to you."

"Hell!" the man snarled. "What're you talkin' about? Wasn't it me left that knife for you?"

"I got to admit. It did help. It only took me all the rest of that day to roll over to it and cut myself loose. There's slashes on my wrists I got cutting the rawhide. You could sure as hell have made it a lot easier."

"You did get loose, and I'm the one responsible."

"You expectin' me to thank you?"

"I ain't expectin' nothin'," the man asserted coldly, his eyes going crafty. "But I don't see why we can't let bygones be bygones."

"You'd like that."

"Think it over. Besides," he went on, moistening lips hopefully, "I maybe got something you want."

"Yeah? What's that."

"First off, I say we go over in the shade, where my horse is, get out of this damned sun."

Dillon glanced over at Harlow. Harlow shrugged. Dillon looked back at the man. "What's your name, mister?"

"Jason Tanner."

"Okay, Tanner, let's get some shade."

Tanner turned and walked back into the rocks,

Dillon and Harlow following after him on their horses. Tanner had found a grassy spot surrounded by boulders as high as or higher than a man's head. As Tanner halted beside his horse, Dillon saw that Tanner was riding Slade's horse.

"You're ridin' a dead man's horse," Dillon commented coldly, as he and Harlow dismounted.

Tanner shrugged. "What the hell. He won't be needing it anymore. And another thing. If I wanted to finish you two for good, I could've taken your horses with me when I rode off."

"True enough, I reckon," admitted Dillon. "Now, what's this you got for us."

"I got to be sure you two ain't gonna hold any grudges."

"You ain't in no position to be sure of anything."

"Well, in that case, forget it."

Impatient, and not overly anxious to deal with the son of a bitch, Dillon reached back for his gun, intending only to cover the man. It was a silly move; if he had been more alert, he would not have done it. The moment he lifted his revolver from its holster, Tanner—with the speed of a striking rattler—drew his own weapon and fired wildly at them both, ducking out of sight behind a boulder.

Beside Dillon, Harlow gasped, "Aw, shit, Dillon, I'm hit!"

Dillon saw Harlow drop to the ground and begin twisting slowly. Tanner ducked out from the other side of the boulder and sent a second round at Dillon, this slug searing past Dillon's ear and ricocheting off the rock wall behind him. Dillon fired back at him twice, but Tanner was already scuttling off among the rocks.

Dillon looked down at Harlow. Blood was pouring from a wound in the little fat man's side; his face was ashen with fear as he stared wide-eyed up at Dillon.

"You got to help me, Dillon!" he pleaded.

"I'll finish off this bastard. That's a promise."

"Never mind him. Help me!"

Tanner appeared then, at least fifty yards further down the arroyo, crouching on the top of a boulder that gave him an excellent view of Dillon and Harlow. From that vantage point he had them cold. Dillon ducked out of sight against the flank of a boulder. Peering carefully around it at Tanner, Dillon saw the man waiting, his gun out and ready.

"You goin' to put that gun away, mister?" Tanner called.

"You already shot my buddy!"

"You drew on me first."

"All right. All right. Hold off. We'll deal."

"Throw your gun out."

"I ain't throwin' no gun out."

"Then it's a standoff."

"No, it ain't. I got your horse here. And your canteens filled with water. You can't go nowhere without a horse, so fry out there, if you want. I ain't in no hurry."

"All right. We'll deal."

"What you got that's so important?"

Dillon saw him moisten his lips and slowly lower his gun. "The map. I took it from the girl."

"The map to that mine? Where the gold's hid?"

"That's the one."

"What was all that shootin' about?"

"I was shootin' at the girl. She was leading me to the mine, but she broke fast and left me in the dust."

"If you got the map why'd you need her?"

"I don't know this country—couldn't read the map. But she could. I was makin' her lead me to it."

"You never should've trusted her."

"I know that now, dammit!"

"Show me the map."

Tanner fumbled in his vest pocket, then took out the map. Unfolding it with a single flip of his left hand, he held it up so Dillon could see it.

"You're too far away. Put down your gun and come closer."

"Throw your gun out."

With a shrug, Dillon threw the revolver onto an open space a few yards from him.

"Now, step out in plain sight."

Dillon did as Tanner told him. Tanner studied him for a minute longer, then jumped down from the boulder and, keeping Dillon in sight, approached carefully, his six-gun leveled on him.

Behind Dillon, Harlow gasped, "Damn you, Dillon! What about me?"

Dillon snarled, "Stay put. I'll handle this."

"That's easy for you to say. I got a hole in me."

"There ain't nothin' I can do about that."

"Get out of my way," Harlow croaked. "I'll kill the bastard when he shows."

"Sure," Dillon said, stepping to one side.

A second later, as Tanner stepped into the small

69

area behind the boulder where Dillon waited, Harlow raised his gun, his hand shaking. Tanner seemed to have expected it. He fired down at Harlow twice, the first slug destroying his face, the other one pounding his shoulder into the ground.

Then he swung the gun up to cover Dillon. "Damn your eyes, mister. You knew he was going to do that!"

"That's right. And I knew what you'd do when he tried it."

"He could've killed me."

"That's right. Then I'd have the map all to myself."

"You're a cold-blooded bastard."

Dillon shrugged. "You didn't seem to blink much just now."

"No," Tanner said, "I didn't, at that. I been out of action for a while. Just broke out of Leavenworth. When that bitch lit out on me just now, I figure I got my edge back."

Waggling his gun at Dillon to make him step back, Tanner bent, took the gun out of the dead man's hand, and stuck it into his belt. Then he stepped cautiously away from Dillon and lowered his six-gun. "You know my name, mister. What's yours?"

"Sam Dillon."

Tanner took out the map and handed it to Dillon. "You know this country, I reckon. Here's the map. Which way do we go now?"

Dillon puzzled over the map a moment or two, his palm scratching his unshaven face, his one eye narrowed. He turned the map upside down, peered at it some more, shook his head, then handed it back to Tanner.

"Hell," he said, "this here ain't got no markin's on it that I can see. Ain't even any indication which way is north."

"There's a river traced on it."

"That's what it looks like, but it sure don't resemble any river I know of around here. And there's a peak in it I can't place. Less'n it's out of this here badlands."

"Shit," said Tanner, lifting his six-gun. "You ain't no help."

Dillon took a quick step back, raising his hands. "Hey, now, watch it, Tanner. Careful with that gun."

"If you can't help me, what do I need you for?"

"Then ride off. Let me be."

"If I'm going to overtake that Apache wildcat, your horse will come in handy. This is tough country for horses and men alike."

"Take Harlow's horse. You're welcome to it."

Tanner grinned, like he was chewing on a nest of yellow jackets. "Two horses would be even better. Don't worry," he said, lifting the gun, "I'll place the bullet real careful."

Dillon knew the son of a bitch was serious. He took a quick step back. "Hey, listen. Let me see that map again. Maybe we can work somethin' out on this."

"Work something out?"

"Sure."

Tanner grinned. "You were holding out on me. You can read the map."

"No, I can't. I ain't lyin' about that."

"Then what're you offering?"

"I know an Indian. An old Navajo. Lives in Red Rock. Grew up in this country. Hell, these rocks talk to him. He's been out with prospectors and never yet failed to bring a party back. He'd know where that lost mine is—once he got a good look at the map."

Tanner frowned, considering the possibility. "What'll it cost us?"

Dillon grinned. "Hell, this one'll do anything for a pint of whiskey."

"That's all it would take, huh?"

Dillon nodded. He had been talking fast, praying Tanner would go for it. The thing was, Dillon wasn't lying. This Navajo was as old as Methuselah and knew this country better than the scorpions and rattlers that owned it.

Tanner lowered his gun. He smiled again, that crooked-toothed grin that sent a shudder up Sam Dillon's spine. "I wasn't goin' to pull this here trigger," he told Dillon. "I just wanted to make you concentrate. Figured you might be holding out on me. I say we ride in to Red Rock and look up this here Navajo. How's that sound, partner?"

"Sure," Dillon said, taking a deep breath.

"Course I'll have to keep an eye on you." Tanner walked over to where Dillon had thrown his Colt and stuck it in his belt alongside Harlow's. "So you won't be needing this."

Sam Dillon allowed himself a smile. "Hell, no. Not unless we run into an Apache war party."

"And that ain't likely this far north."

"Just what I was thinking."

• . . •

That morning Longarm had read the tracks leaving the campsite and had seen at once what must have happened. Someone had intruded on the camp early that morning and Opal, for some reason, had ridden off with him. Retrieving his horse, he'd taken after the two riders; but a little while ago he'd lost the tracks in a gravel streambed and had been forced to backtrack in order to find the spot where they'd left it—a stretch of caprock that led out of the canyon onto a barren, scrub-pocked flat.

Then came the shots—three of them in rapid succession, their crackling echo seeming to come from a low tumble of rocks and buttes a half mile or so ahead of him. He spurred immediately toward them, and was just entering the rocks when he heard the pounding of hooves off to his right. He turned his mount in that direction and saw Opal galloping along the base of a cliff. She was hanging forward over the neck of her mount, and he could tell at once that she was having difficulty staying in the saddle. Taking after her, he lost sight of her in the rocks beyond the cliff, but kept going until he caught her spoor.

Fresh blood.

When he caught up to her, she had dismounted and was huddling in the shade provided by a few boulders, her horse cropping the grass a few yards away. As he rode up, she roused herself and tried to get back up onto her feet, but could not manage it. Dismounting quickly, he knelt by her. Her blouse was dark with her blood and he could see the hole in it left by the exiting bullet. It looked as if she had been shot from behind, the bullet tearing clear through her.

Her eyes opened and, when she saw it was Longarm, she managed a faint smile of pure relief.

"What happened?" he demanded. "Who did this?"

"It is so long a story," she said. "This man shoot me. He was very lucky. He miss me but the bullet ricochet."

He tore away a strip of her skirt and bound her as tightly as he could to stem the bleeding. It seemed to help some.

"Can you ride?" he asked.

"Yes. But I rest now for little while."

"You need a doctor, Opal," he told her, "and sooner rather than later. Is there any place nearby where we can find one?"

"Red Rock. There is doctor there."

"What's his name?"

She shrugged. "I dunno. Doc is what we all call him."

"How far is it?"

"Ten, maybe fifteen miles."

"Do you think you can make it that far?"

"I can if you will help me."

"Of course I'll help you. This doctor. Is he any good?"

"He is a man with death in his eyes. He drinks and coughs much. It is not pleasant to hear him. But he is gentle to the women when the midwives ask him to help. And he is good with the bullet wounds. Once I see him take a bullet from a man's chest. He operate on top of the bar, and the bar-keeps hold lamps high in the air so he can see."

"Did the wounded man survive?"

"No, but it was a fine operation. Everyone get drunk afterward."

He gave her water from his canteen and decided resting up awhile certainly couldn't hurt, especially when he saw that he had managed to stop the blood flow from her wounds.

An hour later Opal pronounced herself sufficiently rested. They mounted up and rode out. Opal kept just ahead of him to keep them on course, since only she knew the way out of this wilderness of rock and scrubland. Meanwhile, Opal had explained to him what had happened that morning when she went for her horse and why she had not cried out or made any effort to bring him into it.

She also revealed that, though Tanner had been completely unaware of it, she had not been following the map to the mine, but was moving in a wide circle that she hoped would bring her back onto her trail—and Longarm. She'd had little doubt that he would have taken after her as soon as he woke up. Unfortunately, she had been impatient to rid herself of Tanner, and when she saw her chance to make a break, had taken it. Had not her luck run out, she told him, she was certain she would have escaped cleanly. It was of no consequence to her that Tanner now had the map. It would do him little good, and she had no doubt she would be able to find the mine without the map.

That the man who had taken her by surprise was Jason Tanner should have surprised Longarm, but it didn't. He had followed Tanner into these badlands and knew Tanner must still be around somewhere; naturally, the first sign of life—such as smoke from their camp fire—had drawn him like a bee to honey.

Now, as they rode, Longarm kept an alert eye on Opal and could not help noticing how much larger the bloodstain on her bandage had become. Though Opal kept herself upright as she rode and uttered not a word of complaint, he could see that under the sun's relentless hammer she was wilting rapidly.

He was beginning to wonder if they would ever be able to put this blistering wasteland behind them. On all sides of them titanic rock forms towered, some on the distant horizon, others looming intimidatingly close. Many of them resembled monstrous beasts of an earlier time congealed in stone. Some of the rock faces were a scalded red, others yellow, while still others gleamed like great washed veins of coal.

They were riding through a broad, steep-sided canyon when Longarm noticed that the sun was partially obscured by a rack of clouds that seemed to have materialized out of nothing in the relentlessly bright sky. A chill wind brushed over them and then was gone, after which the sun's awful weight seemed to lean on them all the more heavily.

"Feel that breeze?" he asked Opal.

She nodded and turning carefully in her saddle, smiled wanly at him.

Thunder rumbled like distant cannons. The cloud overhead was building rapidly now, and deep in its dark vaults he glimpsed lightning flickering—like the smile of some titanic weather god. Longarm's horse flattened its ears as the thunder's ominous mutter began to rumble off the canyon's walls. He patted the animal to calm it, and felt a sudden damp wind brushing the back of his neck; the horse's mane suddenly stood straight up.

A second later came the first drops of rain.

"Better dig out your slicker!" he called to Opal.

She tried to reach back for it as she rode, but without much luck.

"Hold up," he told her. "I'll give you a hand."

She reined in her horse, then sagged wearily forward in her saddle as he dismounted, untied her slicker, and handed it up to her. She was unable to get her arms into it, so he suggested she button the top buttons and drape the slicker over her shoulders like a cape. She did as he suggested; he put on his own slicker and stepped back up into his saddle, glancing skyward as he did so.

The thunderhead had now spread its dark tendrils over the entire sky, and the rain increased, falling now in big, scattered drops. The storm could still pass over harmlessly, Longarm realized, but it was not likely. Longarm was betting on a fearful downpour—maybe even a cloudburst.

"Let's ride," he called to Opal. "We got to find a way out of this canyon."

Even as he spoke, the wind came, shoving at him like a palpable, urgent hand, after which came the sound of rain beating the ground behind them, the sound of it rising to a fierce crescendo as it overtook them, striking Longarm with a violence and a suddenness that almost took his breath away. His horse stumbled slightly, but regained its balance swiftly, and Longarm gave the animal its head. The horse lifted to a gallop and plunged on down the canyon. Thunder rolled and crashed about them, and lightning snapped, the sound of it like whips cracking, the smell of it mingled with the dusty odor stirred up by the stinging, lashing tendrils of rain that raked the canyon.

Longarm glanced back to make sure Opal was keeping up with him. She was, but just barely.

The rain pounded and lashed at the two riders, flailing them with maddening insistence. Rain-laden wind squalls surged over them. Already Longarm was sore from the pounding his back was taking, and when he turned again in his saddle to check on Opal, he could barely make her out through the squalling, ropelike curtains of rain that now separated them. Meanwhile, the sound the rain made as it struck the hard ground was almost as intimidating as the crackling forks of lightning that came split seconds after each soul-quaking crash of thunder.

Almost before he was aware of it, he found himself plunging on into a narrow arroyo, its steep, sheer walls closing in on him ominously. He didn't like it. He slowed his horse and forced it to veer over toward the closest rock wall. As he did so, he turned in his saddle and waved to Opal, indicating she should follow him. When he saw her turning her horse in his direction, he looked back at the rock wall, searching for a trail of some sort that would take them out of this.

Already the water swirling down the arroyo was above his mount's fetlocks, its level continuing to rise rapidly. When at last he caught sight of what appeared to be a break in the wall of rock, he flung himself from his horse and, putting his head down, pushed through the pounding rain toward it, pulling his horse after him. When he reached the break in the wall, he was able to make out a series of steplike ledges and above them what appeared to be a game trail leading out of the arroyo.

When Opal rode up behind him, slumped wearily forward over her pommel, he helped her down out of her saddle, took the reins of both horses, and began to haul them up the rock steps after him toward the game trail he had spotted above it. Opal followed. They kept going until he came upon a narrow ledge under a sheltering overhang of rock. They were a good thirty yards above the floor of the arroyo by this time and he was gambling this would be high enough. Going any higher was out of the question by this time. The cloudburst had increased in fury, almost obliterating the trail, and he could barely see the ground beneath his feet.

He helped Opal over to the most level spot he could find under the overhang, then took off his own slicker and placed it on the ground for her. She sat gratefully down upon it, and leaning back against the rock wall, closed her eyes. He could see how desperately weary she was, and found himself wondering how she had managed to keep up with him through that awesome downpour. He tethered the horses to some scrub pine clinging to the canyon's slope, took a blanket from his bedroll, and returned to Opal, covering them both with it as he slumped down beside her.

Despite the brow of rock over their head, the

rain still reached in to pelt them, and the lightning seemed to be probing for them also as it winked and gleamed through the arroyo's rain-shrouded gloom. And then he heard it. Above the ceaseless, thundering rattle of the rain, came another, deeper sound that seemed to cause the great stone walls around them to shudder. A moment later a dark, surging crest of water swept through the arroyo, carrying before it uprooted trees and thundering boulders that bounded ahead of the torrent like loose cannonballs. Behind this debris came the flash flood itself, a muddy, raging torrent of brown, silt-laden water that surged rapidly higher and higher as it swept on past them. Caught between the arroyo's walls as between the walls of a narrowing chute, the surging tide's swirling tendrils almost reached the ledge upon which Longarm and Opal were huddled.

How long the storm continued was difficult to tell. All sense of time was beaten out of them. Like dumb things they watched the torrent sweep past their precarious perches, felt the thunder rock the ground under them, and did their best to ignore the lightning until finally the thunder abated somewhat and the lightning flickered less insistently. Not long after, the roaring rainfall became only a steady, insistent downpour.

The rain continued to slacken and Longarm found he could see pretty well. He left Opal and struggled up to the rim of the arroyo, then returned to her. She was by now too weak to make the climb on foot, and Longarm did not trust their horses on the wet, poorly anchored shale. He slung Opal over his shoulder as gently as he could manage it, then carried her to the rim. Once there, he put her down on the sopping ground, covered her with his blanket, then returned to the ledge to fetch the horses. It took almost twice as long to get the spooked horses up the steep, treacherous trail, but he managed it.

By now it was obvious that Opal would be unable to ride unaided, so he decided to carry her in front of him on his saddle and lead her horse. She did not argue with him when he suggested this course, and was able to provide some help as he pulled her up onto his pommel.

Three hours later, they reached the outskirts of Red Rock. Opal's head was slumped back against Longarm's chest by this time and the only evidence he had that she lived came from the fever he could feel raging through her. It was no longer raining, but the tin roofs of the shacks gleamed and the adobe buildings squatted like mushrooms on the soggy flat. As he put his horse down the slope toward the town, Opal stirred herself enough to direct him away from the town to the northeast, to the valley where Bilcher had built himself a small shack.

It was dark when Longarm rode into the valley and came upon the shack, the bright moonlight outlining it clearly in the folds of a distant hill. Reaching the cabin, he swung down. Carrying Opal to the door, he turned his back to it, rammed the door open, and brought her inside.

He put her down on a bed in the far corner, then went back outside to tend to the horses. A lean-to in the back served as a stable; he unsaddled his horse, but not the horse he had been leading, and found feedbags and some oats under a wooden trough. There was a hand pump outside, and as soon as he had watered both horses and filled their feedbags, he returned to the shack and built a fire in the fireplace.

Then he went over to see to Opal.

She was not conscious. Carefully, he lifted her slender body with his big hands and unwound the bloody bandage. Both the entry and the exit wounds were inflamed and what blood now oozed from them was an evil-looking black. He heated some water in an iron kettle he hung over the fireplace, washed out the wounds, then ripped off another strip from her skirt and bound her up again. When he finished, he stepped away from her cot and peered unhappily down at her. Through it all, she had remained unconscious. He needed to ride into Red Rock to get that doctor she had mentioned earlier.

Longarm stepped closer, took her by the shoulders, and shook her gently. Her eyes fluttered open and she turned her head to look at him. He did not like the flushed, hectic look in her eyes.

"I'm going into Red Rock," he told her. "I'll bring that doctor back with me. Hang on now."

She appeared to nod, then closed her eyes.

He built up the fire in the fireplace, then left.

Chapter 5

The lights of Red Rock gleamed like eyes in the night as he rode toward the town. After the rain, the air was miraculously cool, washed clean and clear. What stars were visible through the broken racks of clouds seemed incredibly close and bright—as if they were being observed through spectacles. Thunder still muttered intermittently in the foothills beyond the town, and lightning flared occasionally in the remaining cloud masses on the horizon.

The plank bridge over the stream was barely high enough to clear the roaring water that even this late still surged under it. Gaining Red Rock's public square, he found it fetlock-deep in clinging mud. The few wooden frame structures fronting the Spanish-style square looked bedraggled and weary, and the adobe huts squatting further back looked even more cheerless. The rain barrels were filled to the brim, he noticed as he clopped past, and two gutters on the more substantial frame dwellings hung from the roofs, their ends buried solidly in the wet ground.

Longarm pulled up in front of the livery, dismounted, and led his horse into it. The old Mexican running the place stepped out of a horse stall and leaned his pitchfork against the wall.

"Go light on the oats," Longarm told him. "And give him a quick rubdown. I'll be right back."

The Mexican took the horse's bridle and nodded. "Two bits, señor."

Longarm flipped a coin at him. "Where can I find the doc?"

"The barbershop, or maybe the saloon across the street. If he ain't there, try the Gold Nugget."

Longarm thanked the man and hurried from the livery. The barbershop was closed and the saloon was a dusty, unhappy place with few men at the bar and no doctor. Back outside on the muddy wooden sidewalk, he peered down the square at the dim glow of yellow light spilling out onto the muddy ground. A piano's tinny tinkle came from that direction and he started for it.

Stepping inside the Gold Nugget, he had no trouble at all spotting the doctor. He was dressed in a black frock coat and trousers and was slumped at a table in the rear, staring blearily at an empty bottle of whiskey, his black leather doctor's bag sitting on the table beside him. Longarm walked over, introduced himself, and sat down.

The doctor's name was Neville Parkhurst. Despite his evident inebriation, he was reasonably presentable. He had dark, neatly combed hair and gray eyes. His face was thin, hollow, and as pale as alabaster. He looked like Death in a Frock Coat, and over his person there hung a sour, whiskey smell.

Noting the empty bottle in front of Parkhurst, Longarm ordered a bottle of fresh whiskey from the Mexican bar girl, then watched Parkhurst fill his shotglass to the brim, edge it carefully over the table to him, and with both hands steadying it, lift it to his lips. With a quick backward tilt of his head, he threw the contents of the shotglass down his throat, then wiped his mouth with the back of his hand and reached for the bottle to refill the glass. The second shot followed the first down his gullet just as rapidly. Obviously feeling much better, the doctor leaned back in his chair.

"You are a generous man, sir. Now, what seems to ail you? If you will forgive the impertinence, I see before me a man fit in all his particulars, clear-eyed, steady—a veritable monument to robust good health."

He would have gone on in that vein, but a sudden fit of coughing caused him to double over and grab a handkerchief from his breast pocket to cover his mouth. The siege lasted awhile, and not until it had passed did Longarm reply.

"It's not me, Doc. A friend of mine's got a bad bullet wound. I think it's infected."

"That so? Where is he?"

"It's a she. Name's Opal. She's out at Bilcher's shack in the valley."

The man's eyebrows shot up. "Opal, is it? That

85

same Apache wench used to work in here?"

"That's the one. You ready to go? We ain't got much time."

"I am afraid the wheel on my buggy is broken, Mr. Long. Can't you bring the girl into town? She has many friends here who would, I am sure, be only too glad to offer her assistance."

"There's no time for that."

"Then what do you suggest?"

"We get a horse from the livery. You can ride out with me."

"In my condition? Why, I might topple from the saddle."

"If you did, I'd throw you right back up into it."

He smiled then—a brilliant smile that warmed his dark countenance. "Why, sir, I do believe you would."

"We're wasting time."

"I don't wish to seem importunate . . . but what about this bottle?"

"It's yours. Take it with you."

"Your generosity, sir, is overwhelming."

With trembling hands, Parkhurst screwed the cap back on the whiskey bottle, then put it into his black bag. He stood up—and started to reel. As he reached out blindly for the table, Longarm grabbed him and held him up. When his head had cleared sufficiently, Longarm led him out of the saloon and across the street to the livery. By the time Longarm had saddled a horse for him and lifted him into the saddle, the doctor had fallen asleep, his shoulders draped over a stall's partition. Longarm shook the man awake and helped him up into his saddle.

Parkhurst took another belt from the bottle, rode out of town with Longarm, and was almost sober when they reached Bilcher's cabin. The fire in the fireplace had almost gone out, but as Parkhurst established immediately, that didn't much matter to Opal. She was on fire with fever.

Longarm found some coal-oil lamps and lit them to give Parkhurst enough light to examine Opal's wounds. Parkhurst obviously did not like what he found. He instructed Longarm to build a fire and boil some water. When Longarm had done so, Parkhurst mixed whiskey with the hot water and began swabbing out both of Opal's wounds. Soon the blood that ran out of the wounds became cleaner, healthier-looking. Opal woke once during the process, crying out softly. But Parkhurst ignored her and kept digging into the wounds until he had cleaned them both out thoroughly. Then he bandaged them with fresh bandages he kept in his black bag, pouring generous dollops of whiskey into each wound before he did so.

When he had finished, Opal woke long enough to ask for water. Parkhurst gave it to her and she dropped off into a deep sleep. He rested his hand on her forehead for a minute, then stepped back from the cot, evidently satisfied.

He glanced at Longarm. "Her fever's broke."

A few moments later he went outside with Longarm and accepted one of Longarm's cheroots.

"She going to be all right?"

"Keep her quiet and keep the bandages clean."

"I'll need that whiskey."

"I'll leave it with you. Dilute it with boiled water when you use it."

"If you say so."

The man began to cough then, violently. Longarm looked away and waited, reflecting that it was too bad the doctor couldn't swab out his lungs with alcohol and hot water—and then realized that that was indeed what the dying man had been attempting to do back there in the saloon.

Only it wasn't working.

It was two days after Longarm had left Red Rock with Parkhurst that Sam Dillon and Tanner rode into town a little before noon. They were sharing a single horse, Dillon having lost his mount in the flash flood that overtook and nearly drowned them. It was late in the day, and they rode on through town to its southern outskirts, pulling up in front of a dismal adobe hut, a broken fence surrounding it. A naked five-year-old kid was playing in the dust, along with a pig, some scraggly chickens, and a goat. The two men stalked across the littered yard and entered the adobe without knocking.

An incredibly fat woman was making tortillas over an open hearth. She was stooped double as she worked, but turned and came upright as the two men halted on the other side of the table.

"Where's Santoro?" Sam Dillon asked.

The big woman shrugged her massive frame, her black eyes regarding the two men impassively.

"What're you mean you don't know?"

The woman turned her back on them and went back to mixing the tortillas. Before Dillon could advance on her and fling her around, the doorway behind them darkened and a heavyset Navajo entered, his braided hair reaching almost to his round waist. He was wearing Levi's, a torn leather vest, and a sombrero. This was Santoro.

"What you want?" he asked, crossing the room to place himself between his woman and the two men.

"You," said Dillon. He handed the Indian the map. "Take us to that spot, the canyon marked with the x."

The Indian took the map and studied it intently for a moment or two, then shrugged and handed it back, saying, "I know this canyon. It is called Diablo Canyon. I will take you."

"How much?"

"Fifty dollar. Gold."

"Shit. We ain't got that," said Jason Tanner.

Dillon looked back at Santoro. "We'll have it for you when we get to that mine. There'll be plenty for all of us."

"Ten dollar now—for my woman when I go from here."

"We ain't got that neither," said Dillon.

"Then Santoro not go."

"Goddammit, Santoro," said Dillon, "you're going!"

The Indian walked over to a corner of the room, lifted a shotgun, and leveled it at the two men. "Santoro not go."

"Jesus," said Dillon. "Put that down, Santoro. You kill a white man and they'll string you up."

The Indian shrugged. "Santoro not care. He old man now."

"Look, I'll go buy us some whiskey, Santoro," said Dillon, heading for the door, his gaze on the twin muzzles of Santoro's shotgun. "Then I'll come back and we can discuss this reasonable."

The Indian leaned the shotgun against the wall, and as the two men left he said, "Santoro still want ten dollar first."

"All right," snarled Tanner as he followed Dillon out of the hut, "we heard you."

An hour later in the Gold Nugget, Tanner leaned back in his chair and eyed Sam unhappily. "You said all it would take is a bottle of whiskey."

"He's gettin' independent in his old age."

"Why not let me work that bastard over?"

"You must be crazy. He'd take us back into them mountains and lose us for good. Then where'd we be?"

"All right. We'll get to him through his woman."

"You mean take her as hostage?"

"Something like that."

"There's only one thing wrong with that."

"Yeah?"

"Santoro would just go out and get himself another squaw. They don't put no store by their squaws. As far as they're concerned, one's as good as another."

"I don't think so. See how he planted himself between us and his woman when he walked in?"

"I still don't think it's such a good idea."

"All right. We'll take him this here bottle of

sheep-dip and see if that'll bring him around."

"Be better if we had the ten dollars."

"I know that, dammit, but we don't—and that's the end of it."

The two men got up. Tanner snatched up the bottle of whiskey and the two men left the saloon. A few minutes later, dismounting in front of Santoro's adobe hut, they noticed how quiet the place was. The naked kid was missing and the door of the adobe hung open.

They tramped inside and looked around.

Santoro and his woman were gone.

"The son of a bitch," said Dillon, "they've lit out."

"To Diablo Canyon," Tanner reminded his partner. "Him and his woman and the brat. Now he knows where the mine is, he figures he might as well find it himself."

"Son of a bitch. I never figured on that."

"So I say we take after them."

"Sure. Go ahead. You think you can track an Indian in that country? He'll hang you out to dry the moment he sees you tailing him."

"Then what're we goin' to do?"

"Wait until that bastard comes back with the gold. If he gets it."

"Suppose he don't come back here when he does."

"It's a chance we'll just have to take."

Dillon unstoppered the bottle of rotgut they had purchased for Santoro and took a long swig, after which he handed the bottle to Tanner, who took just as hefty a belt and handed it back. Then they left the hut, mounted up, and rode back to the Gold Nugget.

It was still early and when they entered the saloon, it was empty except for the doc settling into a chair at the rear of the place. He had a fresh bottle sitting on the table beside him and a deck of cards in his hands, which he was shuffling as he looked around hopefully for someone to join him in a game. When he saw Dillon and Tanner enter, he greeted Dillon, then waved both men over.

With nothing else to do, the two men strode over to the table and joined Parkhurst in a poker game.

A little before sundown the same day, while Opal and Longarm were sitting in the yard outside the shack, Parkhurst rode up, obviously agitated.

"Now don't get all riled," said Longarm with a smile. "Opal insisted on getting up. She's been cooped up inside all day."

"It's not that," said Parkhurst, dismounting quickly and hurrying toward them.

"Then what is it?"

"Trouble, the way I see it. But maybe I'm wrong."

"Speak plain, Parkhurst."

"I just finished a poker game in the Gold Nugget with two men who rode in this morning. One of them I knew already. He's been hanging around Red Rock for close to a year now. His name's Sam Dillon."

"His face stove in and he wears an eye patch?"

"That's him, all right."

"And the other one?"

"A thin man with cold eyes and a colder smile."

"That would be Jason Tanner."

"Yes, that's his name. It is as I thought then. You know them both."

"Yes," Longarm replied grimly.

"And so do I," said Opal.

"Then I am afraid I have done you both a disservice," the doctor said unhappily.

"What do you mean?"

"Before I had any idea what they were about, I admitted to having taken care of Opal here. The two seemed to come alive pretty fast when I mentioned her. When I saw the glances they exchanged, I realized I had spoken out of turn. So I lost a few hands and meanwhile got them as drunk as I could, then rode out here."

"What condition are they in?"

"They were sleeping it off facedown on the table when I left. But I don't know how long it'll take for them to shake off the booze."

"You say there were only two of them?" Longarm asked.

"That's right. From what I could gather, they had a map they'd been looking for, and had come to Red Rock to get Santoro to take them to a canyon marked off on it; but Santoro lit out."

Opal smiled at Longarm. "You see? This map, it does them no good."

Longarm got to his feet. "Doc, you think you could stay here and look after Opal? I'm going into town."

"After those two?"

"It's Tanner I want."

93

"They are hard men," Parkhurst warned him. "Dangerous."

"I know that. That's why I'd like to get to them before they come around—and ride out here looking for Opal."

A moment later, as Longarm rode out, Opal appeared in the doorway. She waved. He waved back. Behind her in the doorway Parkhurst stood, a rifle in his hand. As Longarm booted his mount on down the valley, he found himself hoping that the doctor knew how to handle a rifle as well as he did a bottle.

It was dark when Longarm reached Red Rock, but he kept to the hills and rode past the town, then cut down toward the town's backside, avoiding the wooden plank bridge and splashing through the creek behind the town's main square. Dismounting, he tethered his horse to a back fence, passed on through an alley, came out onto the town square, and kept moving along the wooden sidewalk until he came to the Gold Nugget.

Stepping through the batwings, he paused. The saloon's patrons glanced over at him, and for a moment the long, smoke-filled room was almost perfectly quiet. A high-pitched laugh of a Mexican bar girl sitting on a customer's lap in the back cut through the silence. Longarm pushed himself on into the saloon and bellied up to the bar between two swarthy customers. The noise level in the place rose back to its normal level. Longarm purchased a shot of whiskey and mentioned to the barkeep that he was looking for Sam Dillon.

"You a lawman?"

Longarm nodded.

The two men at the bar alongside Longarm heard the barkeep's query and Longarm's response. At once the two sidled away from Longarm, taking their beer with them.

"Him and his buddy's outside," the barkeep said, his eyes shifting unhappily. Why was it, Longarm wondered, that perfectly law-abiding citizens got nervous when talking to him?

"Outside you say?"

The barkeep began polishing the top of the bar. "Yeah. In the alley. Sleepin' it off. They really tied one on this afternoon. Crazy bastards tried to drink the doc under the table."

"Thanks."

"Yeah."

The barkeep moved away to serve another customer. Longarm downed the shot and headed for the saloon's back door. Stepping out through it, he saw no one in the alley. If the two men had been dumped into it, they had long since sobered up and dragged themselves off. Longarm didn't like that. He didn't want those two loose—not if they were anxious to get Opal.

He went back inside and returned to the bar. He waved the barkeep over. "They're not out there," he told the man.

"So what d'you want me to do, lawman?"

"Where are they stayin' in town?"

"How the hell should I know?"

Longarm looked around the saloon. It had quieted the moment he came back inside. By this time, Longarm knew, everyone in the place knew he was a lawman after Tanner and Sam Dillon. He cleared his throat and announced, "I'll give ten dollars in gold to the man who goes after them two and tells them I'm in here waitin' for them."

"You crazy, mister?" the barkeep behind him asked. "Them two'll kill you."

"You mean they'll try."

"I don't want no gunplay in here!"

"Don't worry. Soon's they get here, we'll go outside."

A small man with sunken cheeks wearing a frayed buckskin jacket grabbed his hat and dashed from the saloon. As the sound of his booted feet faded on the wooden sidewalk, Longarm turned back to the barkeep, bought himself a bottle of whiskey, and took it with him over to a table against the wall. He sat down, filled his glass, and leaned his head back against the wall to wait.

It would be one man against two—odds sure to lure a man like Tanner, if he and the other were still in town.

He was on his second glass when the fellow in the buckskin burst into the saloon. "They're on the way," he called over to Longarm. "I caught them at the bridge riding out."

"Thanks, mister," Longarm said.

He left the table and walked to the batwings and peered out. As he saw the two men riding across the square toward the saloon, he flipped a coin at the man and pushed through the batwings.

The fellow in the buckskin came out after him. "You . . . you want any help, lawman?"

"Stay out of this. You done enough already."

"You can't take these two alone."

Longarm was losing patience with his would-be sidekick. "Just don't get in my line of fire."

The man ducked hastily back into the saloon. Longarm moved down the sidewalk, his eyes on the two approaching horsemen. Both men's faces were lost in the shadows of their hat brims, but Longarm had little trouble distinguishing between the two. He was sure his own figure stood out clearly enough against the adobe building, its surface bright in the moonlight, but his intentions were to use this to lure the two riders closer.

At the head of an alley that ran alongside the saloon, he stopped and faced the approaching riders.

They pulled up cautiously.

"That you, Longarm?" Jason Tanner called softly.

Longarm could see the gleam of their two revolvers. "It's me, all right, Tanner. Nice of you to oblige me like this."

"Thought you'd appreciate it."

"You can stay out of this, if you want, Dillon. It's Tanner I'm after."

"Thanks, lawman, but I'm invitin' myself in. I ain't forgetting you was willing to let me rot in that mine shaft."

"Shame you didn't."

Longarm saw the movement of their gun barrels and ducked down the alley, legging it hard. Two shots whined off the adobe building's walls, and then came the sudden pounding of their horses as the two men galloped into the alley after him. Longarm ducked into the alley running behind the saloon and flattened himself against the wall.

The two riders charged past him, then pulled up, hesitating, not sure which direction Longarm had taken.

"Over here, Tanner," Longarm called softly, firing at the man as he did so.

But a split second before Longarm spoke up, Tanner ducked low over his horse and swung it around. Longarm's shot missed. Both riders charged at Longarm then, their six-guns blazing. Keeping low, Longarm stood his ground for a moment and returned their fire, saw one of them throw up his arms and peel backward off his horse, then turned and raced down the alley, the remaining rider firing a rapid volley after him, the slugs ricocheting off the buildings and back-porch railings.

Still running flat out, Longarm fired back over his shoulder at the horse and rider closing on him. The pounding hooves increased their thunder. Longarm drove to one side. He was not fast enough. The chest of the horse caught the back of his shoulder and knocked him violently to one side. He slammed headfirst into a wall. The pounding hooves faded as the rider swept on past him and he crumpled to the ground, barely conscious. He hit the alley floor and remembered nothing more.

Chapter 6

Longarm opened his eyes and looked up at the barkeep bending over him. Beside the barkeep was the little fellow with the buckskin jacket who had run off so eagerly to fetch Tanner and Dillon. The alley behind them was lit by lanterns in the hands of many of the curious crowding around them.

"Thanks, mister," said the barkeep.

"What for?" Longarm asked, sitting up and rubbing the painful knob on his head where it had stuck the unyielding adobe wall.

"For not shooting up my saloon—and for my horse. Dillon and that other one with him took fresh horses from the livery, and one of them was my black. Now I got him back."

"The bastards flattened Miguel too," said the little one.

Looking closer at him, Longarm saw he was a Mexican. He had a round, pleasant face with a thin mustache and sharp, honest eyes. "Miguel is the hostler?" Longarm asked him.

"*Sí, señor.*" He took Longarm's hand and helped him to his feet. "They leave him with a bad gash in the head."

Bracing himself against the wall, Longarm said, "I got one of them. Which was it?"

The barkeep answered: "Sam Dillon."

"Right through that eye patch," the Mexican said. "Your bullet, he push the patch right out the back of his head."

"What about the other one?"

"He get away, señor."

"Did I wing him?"

The little fellow shook his head. "I do not think so."

"Not from the way he rode out of here," agreed the saloon owner, standing nearby.

The owner of the saloon and the Mexican helped Longarm through the crowd, then into the saloon, where he was led to a corner table. The Mexican helped Longarm into a seat, then sat down beside him. The barkeep brought Longarm a fresh bottle of whiskey and poured a drink for him. Longarm thanked the man and tossed the whiskey down. The hushed crowd that had followed them into the saloon began to thin out after that, and Longarm glanced over at the little Mexican in the buckskin jacket, recalling how eagerly the fellow had rushed off to bring back Tanner and Dillon.

"What's your name?" Longarm asked him.

"José."

"What's your interest in all this, José? You sure as hell didn't waste any time going after them two."

His smile was disarming. With a shrug, he explained, "It is very simple, señor. I am a coward."

"Most men are. But you did offer to side me, don't forget. Besides, in your case I figure there's more to it than that."

He sighed. "I had a sister, señor. She was most fearfully ravaged by that one-eyed devil you kill. Sam Dillon. But when I seek to avenge my sister's honor, he beat me with the barrel of his gun. And from then on, he treat me very badly."

"So you had a grudge."

"All day and every night I think of only one thing—this terrible gringo's death. It is all I want. Even in church do I pray for this thing."

"And that's why you went after them two."

"*Sí*, señor." He brightened at once. "And you answer José's prayer. You kill the gringo Dillon. I think you very great man."

"No," said Longarm wearily. "Just a lucky one. I was shooting blind in that alley, hoping to get them both."

Longarm filled his glass and downed its contents as quickly as before, then leaned back. His head was still spinning from the blow it took. He pushed the bottle toward José. The little man shook his head.

"What you do now, señor?" he asked.

"Go after the other one."

"That is what I think too. And, señor, when you go after him, I will ride with you."

"You just admitted to being a coward, didn't you, José?"

"That is true, señor."

"I can't risk it, José. In this business, a coward's as dangerous as a Colt without a firing pin."

"But I want no longer to be a coward."

"You think you can manage that, do you?"

"I will follow your example."

"Hell, when I look down the bore of a .44, I'm just as scared as the next man."

"But you do not show it, señor."

"Yeah, well, I guess that's the trick to it. Be as scared as you want. Just don't show it."

"I will do that, then."

"It ain't easy. And you might end up eating lead. Jason Tanner has already killed more than his share."

"Tanner? That is the other one?"

"Yeah. He just broke out of prison."

"José will ride beside you," he announced proudly, "and together we will bring in this man."

Longarm shrugged, too weary to argue with José any longer. "My horse is tied out back," he said. "Take care of it for me, then saddle a horse for yourself. We'll be out of here soon's I can stop this buzzin' in my head."

José nodded eagerly and hurried from the saloon. Longarm poured himself another drink, pulled it toward him—then pushed it away decisively and rested his head back against the wall and closed his eyes.

He didn't really need another drink. All he needed right now was a clear head and a few minutes' rest.

● ● ●

Longarm caught sight of what must have been Tanner's horse tethered in a draw behind the shack. Dismounting, he told José to stay back and cover him. Then he drew his .44, angled down the slope to the shack, and peered in through one of the windows.

A lantern hanging from a rafter cast a dim light over the one-room interior. A small fire crackled in the fireplace. Opal was sitting at the kitchen table with Parkhurst; the two of them were playing cards, for Christ's sake! Both had their backs to him, so he couldn't get their attention without making a racket.

If Tanner was nearby, he must still be making his approach to the shack. But what the hell was keeping him? Maybe one of Longarm's wild shots had winged the bastard. Longarm glanced quickly around him, his eyes looking for movement of any kind, but the moonlit landscape revealed nothing. He looked up the slope where he had left José. There was not enough light for Longarm to see him, but he assumed José could see *him* against the lit window. He raised his arm and waved him on down, then listened until he could hear José picking his way down the steep slope before moving to the shack's door and nudging it open.

Opal and Parkhurst turned. What he saw on their faces warned him, but not soon enough as he felt the muzzle of Tanner's Colt dig into the small of his back. The man snatched Longarm's Colt out of his hand and flung it into a corner of the shack. Then he rammed the muzzle of his Colt deeper into Longarm's back and propelled him roughly into the shack. The man had been flattened against the wall just inside the door, out of Longarm's line of sight when he peered through the window.

Longarm came to a halt against the table and turned.

Tanner was grinning at him. "You made quite a racket comin' down that hill," he said. "I been expectin' you. What took you so long?"

Longarm didn't bother to answer the man.

On his feet beside Longarm, Parkhurst spoke up. "Sorry I couldn't warn you, Long. He heard you coming and threatened to kill Opal if either one of us made a sound."

"Never mind," said Longarm. "I should've been more careful."

"Yep," agreed Tanner, smiling wolfishly. "You sure as hell were careless. I should kill you, seeing as how you shot down my pal. But I'll let it go at that. Opal said if I killed you, she wouldn't take me to that mine shaft in Diablo Canyon, the one where all the gold's hid. And she's got enough Apache blood in her, so I believe her."

"She still won't take you to that canyon, Tanner."

"Sure, she will—when she sees me begin to pick you apart with this gun. A toe here, a finger there. Just little pieces. That'll convince her."

"How you going to handle the two of us? You'll have to sleep some. Then we'll nail you."

"I can handle it," he said cockily. "Don't you worry none about that. You give me any trouble and I'll take it out on this here Apache bitch. Don't forget, she's wounded already."

"Bastard!" Opal said.

He walked over to her and slapped her as hard as he could. At that moment the door behind him swung wide and José, his face frozen with fear, stepped inside, his rifle at the ready. Tanner reacted like an uncoiling snake. He grabbed Opal and flung her up in front of him, using her as a shield. José froze. Parkhurst flung himself to the floor and snatched up Longarm's Colt and fired at Tanner's back. He missed, but Tanner turned and fired down at him, planting two holes in the doctor's chest; then he snatched the rifle out of José's hand, brushed him contemptuously aside, and bolted out through the door, dragging Opal after him into the darkness.

As Longarm plucked his Colt from Parkhurst's fingers and started through the door after Tanner, a shot from the darkness took out a piece of the door frame an inch over his head. Longarm ducked quickly back inside and slammed the door.

"I got the cabin covered, Longarm," Tanner called. "The first one shows in that doorway, I'll ventilate."

"José!" Longarm said. "Put out that lamp."

As José jumped up onto a chair to take down the lamp, a bullet crashed through the window. The lamp exploded, sending shards of flame over the floor and the wall beyond. Flinging up his arm to protect his eyes, José beat out the flames with his hat as Longarm stomped out the fire in the fireplace, then flung open the door.

A rifle shot slammed into it and ricocheted past Longarm into the shack's interior, shattering a window behind them.

"He can see you!" Opal cried. "Get back inside!"

Longarm flung the door shut just as Tanner sent another round at him, this one punching a hole in the flimsy door and slamming across the top of the table.

"Opal!" Longarm cried through the door. "Break away! He can't follow you in the dark!"

"No, I cannot do this!"

"She'll be all right, Longarm," Tanner called, "long as she does what I tell her."

"I will be all right, Custis!" Opal called. "Do not worry! I take him to the gold. Then he let me go."

Cursing in frustration, Longarm slipped the door open a crack. But the moon had vanished behind a rack of clouds and he could see nothing; a moment later he heard the pounding of hooves as Tanner and Opal rode off into the night.

They found another lamp and lit it, then rebuilt the fire. Parkhurst was in bad shape. With José's help, Longarm carried the man over to the cot. But when they tried to lay him flat, he insisted on sitting up. For a dying man he seemed astonishingly alive, his eyes gleaming with what could only be described as expectation, happy expectation.

When Longarm pulled up a chair beside the cot and tried to inspect the two bullet holes in his chest, Parkhurst pushed his hands away. "I'm the physician here," he told Longarm. "Allow me to treat the patient."

"You're in no condition to do that."

"In that case I propose we let nature take its course."

"That's crazy."

"For you, maybe. But not for me."

A moment later, when Parkhurst began to lose consciousness, Longarm pulled the man gently down onto the cot and pushed his head back onto a pillow. Then he asked José to bring over a blanket. As Longarm was pulling it up over Parkhurst's ruined chest, the doctor opened his eyes, and in that instant Longarm understood what Opal meant by saying she had seen death in Parkhurst's eyes.

Parkhurst smiled up at Longarm. "The heaviness in my chest is easing, Long. My head is growing lighter. It seems I am on my way, friend."

He meant he was dying—which would cure his rotting lungs for sure, by consigning them to the worms. It was a macabre way of looking at it, but Longarm could not mistake the joy in the man's eyes as he contemplated his upcoming journey.

"I'm sorry about this, Parkhurst," Longarm told him.

"But you shouldn't be, you know."

Standing beside Longarm, José shook his head unhappily. Evidently he had known and liked the doctor. "It is my fault, señor," he said. "If I not come in like that—"

"Nonsense, José," Parkhurst said, turning his head slightly to address him. "One cannot argue with fate—or the gods. The sentence was passed on me a long time ago; only a capricious fate denied me a swift resolution. Now at last my deliverance is at hand."

He began to cough then, a weak, halfhearted series of gasps which brought up only a thin line of blood that traced a path from a corner of his mouth to his chin. Longarm wiped off the blood with his bandanna. The coughing subsided, Parkhurst's head sank back into the pillow, and he closed his eyes.

José pulled up a chair beside Longarm and the two of them kept vigil until dawn. As the first light of day filtered through the shack's broken windows, Parkhurst's head lifted slightly from the pillow, then fell back. He died then as peacefully as an autumn leaf falling from a tree.

Later that morning, José and Longarm buried Parkhurst on a hillock overlooking the shack. As they returned to the cabin, José looked back up at the gravesite and frowned.

"He was a very brave man, señor," he said.

"Yes, José."

"He die so quiet."

"For him it was a deliverance, something he had waited a long time for."

"Is that how you feel about death, señor?"

"Not yet, José. But if I live long enough, who knows?"

"You mean if you live too long."

"Yes."

José shuddered slightly. It was clear that death was a fearsome enigma for him.

"Why don't you go back to Red Rock now, José?" Longarm suggested. "You mentioned something earlier about a sister. Won't she be worried about you?"

"No, señor, she will not be worried."

"Oh?"

"Maria is dead. After that one-eyed animal rape her, she find she carry his child. She does not want this shame, so she drown herself in the river."

Longarm did not see what he could possibly say to comfort the man after such an admission, so he said nothing.

Once they reached the shack, they busied themselves saddling up and packing provisions for their pursuit of Tanner and Opal. When Opal had shouted out that she would take Tanner to the gold and that she would be all right, Longarm had understood perfectly what she was doing at that moment; she was calming down Tanner, doing what she could to make the man ease up.

But that did not mean that she did not want Longarm to follow them.

And thanks to her, Longarm found later that morning, trailing the two of them would not be all that difficult. With a soft, chalklike piece of rock, every few miles or so Opal scratched small arrowlike markers on the face of boulders or rocks.

It was close to dusk, and Longarm had been intent on keeping to the trail they had been following for most of the afternoon, when he caught the distant gleam of a chalk mark on a cliff face off to his right. It was close by the entrance to a narrow canyon. He turned his horse and rode up to it, yanked his hat brim down to shade his eyes from the setting sun, and squinted through its glare at the crooked scrawl. It was another truncated arrow, no more than four or five inches in length. Once again, he could only marvel at Opal's ingenuity in getting this far over to the wall in order to leave the sign.

They rode on into the canyon, its shadowed mouth swallowing them both up and giving them welcome relief from the sun's direct rays. Longarm followed a small stream, no more than a trickle at times, and occasionally disappearing entirely beneath the sand and gravel that floored the canyon. On both sides of them sheer, tawny walls of rock lifted almost straight up, the sky only a thin, bright slash of blue directly over their heads. This twisting, convoluted land seemed designed to catch and hold all those unwary or foolish enough to wander into its rocky embrace. Without those markers left for him by Opal, Longarm would long since have lost his bearings, like those prospectors and settlers whose skeletons he and José had already seen bleaching in the sun. He found himself thinking of that woman he had heard about who had gone mad searching through the Superstition Mountains for the Lost Dutchman's mine. That pile of rocks was no less maddening, no less treacherous, than these badlands. The trouble seemed to be that after a while, exits from canyons or draws became entrances and solid, towering cliff faces appeared abruptly where earlier there had been long, unbroken vistas.

No one truly knew this land, Opal had told him, and he believed her. No one, that is, but the Apaches further south or the Navajo, the only Indians known to have signed a peace treaty with Washington that stuck. This was their land now and they guarded it jealously; so far they had kept their distance but Longarm wondered how long their forbearance would last.

As he and José rode on through the canyon, both men gazed nervously up at the stupendous walls of rock hemming them in. The rock faces were marked by different strata of rock, some forming long, undulating veins of bright amber color, while under or above them ran darker or lighter strata. It was like a giant layer cake through which a titanic meat cleaver had sliced. Great fractures undercut the base of the walls, their cavelike interiors hidden in blue shadow, an indication of the raging torrent this thin trace of a stream became when the snows in the mountains further west melted. Longarm could almost feel the walls thundering as this narrow canyon channeled the spring runoff. In comparison, that cloudburst he had experienced earlier would be only a trickle.

At last, well ahead of them, Longarm saw the canyon walls folding away while the canyon's floor widened almost into a parkland, beyond which he detected a thin, bedraggled line of willows.

"We'll camp in those willows for the night," he told José.

Obviously pleased at the prospect, José nodded, and they kept on through the swiftly gathering dusk. They found that the willows were clustered around a dreary, foul-smelling seep that oozed out of the gravelly soil on the other side of the stream, close by a cliff wall. Dismounting wearily, Longarm decided it would be better for them to obtain their drinking water from the stream itself, rather than the seep. José agreed and they made their camp.

The sun was down by the time they had settled in for the night, their supper jerky, hardtack, and beans washed down with scalding coffee. Afterward, they sat cross-legged before the camp fire, Longarm sharing with José the last of his cheroots.

He was not in a cheerful frame of mind. Before putting down his sleeping blanket, he had searched the area for any sign that Tanner and Opal had camped nearby. He had found none and this bothered him. There was always the chance, of course, that Tanner had camped further into the canyon, some distance from these willows. But even so, the willows would have drawn them, just as they had drawn Longarm and José. Proceeding further into the canyon without taking advantage of this shade—at least for a short rest—did not appear likely; and furthermore, though Longarm and José had covered at least three miles after entering the canyon, Opal had left no more sign for them.

A thought intruded now that he had kept at bay for some time: Tanner might have caught Opal leaving sign for Longarm to follow. If he had, he could then have begun leaving sign of his own, sending Longarm off on the wrong trail.

That could have been what sent them into this canyon. If so, it was not a pleasant thought.

Tanner made camp that night on the crest of a canyon they had been following. The camp fire was blazing but it did little to chase away the chill night wind. Tanner had been glowering at Opal all during the meal, and now he flung the remains of his coffee into the fire and approached her. She was not surprised to see him coming at her like this. His anger had been building all afternoon.

Tanner came to a halt between her and the fire. With the light from the blazing camp fire behind his back, she had difficulty making out the features of his face, but his stance told her all she needed to know.

"All this time I didn't touch you because you was wounded," he told her. "Besides, you was helpin' me get to that canyon so I could get the gold. I figured maybe you were gonna be nice to me when the time came. And then you go and pull a trick like this!"

She said nothing. This gringo was a mad dog. Anything she said would only inflame him further.

He took out of his pocket the soft stone he had taken from her that afternoon and shoved it up to her face. He had caught her leaving a mark for Longarm, had beaten her severely, and then had used the marker to send Longarm off in another direction.

"I want to know," he said. "How long you been doin' this?"

She said nothing.

"Dammit! You goin' to tell me?"

Again she refused to respond. Let the bastard guess how long she had been leaving these signs for Custis. He leaned suddenly forward and slapped her as hard as he could.

"Bitch!" he cried, his voice trembling. "Speak up."

Not wanting to goad him into pure madness,

113

she shrugged and said, "Since we leave the old man's cabin."

"That's what I figured."

She did not respond. Her teeth ached from his last blow.

He straightened up and gazed down at her in some triumph. "Well, he won't be following us so close now. And I sent him on a wild-goose chase this time. Now you ain't got no one but me to comfort you."

Holy Mother of God! This pig was going to comfort her, this filthy son of a whore?

He flung the stone off the cliff, and she thought his face softened a little. He leaned closer. "How's them wounds in your side?"

She shrugged. Twice this day she had almost passed out from the loss of blood still oozing from her wounds. The pain was great and she needed the two holes cleaned out and looked after proper, but she was damned if she was going to let on to this gringo bastard.

"You look well enough to me," he told her, "and its about time you and I got together. I been real patient up till now, but your time's run out, bitch. And you can blame yourself."

Since nothing she could say could possibly make any difference to this gringo pig, she did not reply. Smiling, his teeth yellow showing like fangs in the firelight, he slipped down beside her on her blanket and thrust his face inches from hers. He was expecting her to pull away or make some effort to push him off her, but she waited silently—like death for the hangman.

"You hear me, bitch?" he told her meanly. "We

goin' to make monkey music right here on this blanket. You got to pay for your mistakes in this life."

"And you will pay for this mistake," she spat, unable to contain her contempt for this gringo animal.

"Ah, ha! Will I now?"

He shoved her back onto the blanket, then dropped his body down onto hers, his free hand pushing her dress back. The pain that rocketed through her side caused her to gasp slightly, but he was lost in his own urgency. There was nothing under her dress to hinder his entrance, and she made no effort to do so, turning her head and staring up at the stars, thinking of another place, another time while she let this pig have his rut. It had no meaning for her and she would see to it that it would mean nothing for him too.

When he was done with his rutting, he pulled back, and she could see the vague anger on his face, the awareness that he had not really achieved much more than masturbation. His face hard with disappointment, he looked down at her cold face, the icy contempt in her eyes, and cursing foully, slapped her as hard as he could. Then, pulling up his pants, he got to his feet and walked over to the other side of the camp fire, to return a moment later with the rawhide he used each night to bind her wrists and ankles.

This time he was more than usually brutal as he pulled the rawhide tight, so tight the circulation in her wrists and ankles was immediately cut off. He pulled back and stood up, cursed her again, then spat on her for good measure, and returned to his side of the fire and flung himself down onto his sleeping bag. Her cheek still stinging from the slap, she lifted her head to watch him, then struggled to a sitting position and waited for the sound of his heavy breathing to indicate he had dropped off. She knew what she must do and had been planning this for some time, but always her courage had deserted her at the last moment.

But this final defilement had settled matters for her.

Soon—because of his obscene exertion, she realized grimly—he fell into a deep sleep, his snoring filling the night and echoing off the nearby rocks. Turning her back on the fire, she pushed herself silently as possible across the stony ground until she could feel the camp fire's intense heat beating on her back.

And her bound wrists.

She waited for the fire to die down some—and to get up her courage. Fortunately, Tanner had lately stopped bothering to tie her ankles and wrists together. It gave her more freedom of movement, and she doubted if she would have dared try what she was now contemplating if it would have meant putting her feet into the fire along with her wrists.

Realizing she had waited long enough—that if the flames died down anymore she would probably not be able to burn through the rawhide—she decided it was time. Searching out an ember hot enough to sear through the rawhide, she gritted her teeth, closed her eyes, and thrust her bound wrists into the flame. The pain was so intense, she thought she would cry out. And then she felt one particularly hungry flame licking at the rawhide and held her wrists in this flame for as long as she could. The pain was so great she passed out finally, but not before she yanked her wrists from the fire.

When she awoke later, the searing pain in her wrists was even greater, but when she yanked on the burnt rawhide, it parted as easily as if it had been turned to butter. Pulling her hands around to the front, she gazed down at them. The back of her wrists were blackened; strips of skin—or was it rawhide—hung from them. But not all of the skin had been burnt through, and she could still use her hands.

Swiftly she untied her ankles and then stood up. It was not easy, so tightly had the ankles been bound. She flexed her hands to see how well the fingers would respond. Meanwhile, the pain in her wrists was such that she just wanted to tip her head back and howl.

Instead, she circled the fire. Within reach of Tanner's sleeping form was his rifle, the safety off, a fresh round already cranked into the firing chamber. But she knew her hands did not have the dexterity necessary to snatch the rifle from his grasp, aim it down at the sleeping man, and fire.

But his knife she could handle easily enough.

It was in his sheath, the handle within inches of her own right hand. She kicked the rifle off the rim and, reaching down swiftly, withdrew his knife from its sheath. He stirred, opened his eyes, and looked up at her a moment before she lunged downward with the knife. She felt the blade slip past his vest and into his chest. Its tip struck a rib, twisting the knife out of her hand. It struck the ground and as she grabbed for it, he kicked it away, took her by the neck, and bore her brutally to the ground.

"Bitch!" he cried, his fingers closing about her throat with terrible force. "Bitch!"

She struggled desperately, both hands tugging at his iron fingers. Her head swam. She saw great spots before her eyes and she thought her head was going to explode. Then she felt the strength ebbing from his fingers. He released her and pulled back, seemingly on the verge of passing out. He was losing blood from the knife wound, and realizing his danger, went for his six-gun. But the act of reaching back for it was too painful; it slowed him up, and by the time he was able to clear leather, Opal flung herself forward and snatched the gun from him. There was a brief struggle, and then Opal managed to hurl the gun off into the night.

Then she stepped quickly back away from Tanner. "You can still kill me," she told him. "But if you do, you will die here!"

He staggered to his feet, staring numbly at her, the thick stream of blood pouring from his chest wound.

"You heard me!" she continued. "You will never be able to find your way out of here. You will become prey for the rattlers and scorpions, then food for the vultures. Go ahead, gringo bastard! Kill me if you dare!"

He went down on one knee, his right hand making an effort to stem the blood flowing from his wound. "You—you tried to kill me."

"I'm sorry I did not do it."

"Bitch," he said feebly, his face as white as chalk.

She smiled at him. "Now we are even. We have no weapons. And you are wounded—and so am I."

"What . . . what do you want?"

"A truce."

"Truce?"

"Yes. I will bind your wound and take you to Diablo Canyon. Then you will let me go and you will not touch me again. Ever."

"And if I don't agree?"

"I will abandon you now."

"You need me. You need the supplies I got. The horses."

"And that is why I offer this truce. I am hurt too bad to make it out of here alone. And you need my help."

She could see that Tanner was considering her offer. After a moment he slumped back against a boulder, both hands stemming the flow of blood.

He looked at her warily. "All right," he said, his voice reflecting a grudging respect. "We both don't have no choice. A truce then."

She sat down, the two wounds in her side protesting the sudden movement, the skin hanging in black strips from her wrists, the pain from the burns still so intense she wanted to cry out.

But she had managed to gain a truce, she thought wearily. At least for now.

Chapter 7

The next morning, acting on nothing more than pure instinct, Longarm rode back out of the canyon. José was astonished, but said nothing. It was a long ride and they did not emerge from the canyon's mouth until mid-morning. Longarm sent José in one direction in search of fresh tracks, while he took the other, both of them agreeing to report back to the canyon entrance.

Longarm arrived back at the canyon entrance before José. He had found no sign. But when José rode up, he was waving excitedly. He had found fresh tracks, and took Longarm to the north through the entrance to a long draw and pointed down at the trail. Dismounting, Longarm inspected the hoofprints of two horses, already partially covered by wind-blown sand. Studying them carefully, he found the print of a chipped shoe he had noticed earlier. It was Opal and Tanner, all right.

"Let's get moving," he told José, mounting up, "before the sand wipes out their sign altogether."

As they rode on through the noon hour and into the afternoon, the two men kept their eyes on the ground ahead of them, since they were no longer able to count on any help from Opal. At times they were forced to dismount and lead their horses while peering at the faint trail the two riders were leaving on the hard, sunbaked ground. It was a long afternoon for them, and neither took much time for rest, though they were sure to fill their canteens and water their horses whenever the opportunity arose to do so.

A few hours before sundown they came upon the campsite Opal and Tanner had used the night before. Fanning out around the site of the camp fire, the two men looked for further sign. Inspecting the ashes, Longarm found them not even warm. He looked around, hoping for some indication of which direction Opal and Tanner might have taken when they set out that morning. He found fresh tracks soon enough, tracks that continued along the canyon rim. Peering over the edge into the canyon below him as he rode, Longarm saw the gleam of a rifle barrel resting in the rocks halfway down; the bright gleam meant it had not been there long enough to rust or to be covered by blown sand or dirt. It must have been flung off this rim recently.

He returned to the site of the camp fire and, dismounting, caught what appeared to be a dark bloodstain on a long slab of rock embedded in the ground. He went down on one knee to examine it more closely. The sun had already baked the blood dry, but it was dried blood, all right. To his left, José stood up amidst some rocks and shouted to him. He was holding a six-gun.

Longarm stood up. "How long you figure it's been there, José?"

"It is like new!"

"Let's have a look at it."

José brought it over. Longarm took it and examined it carefully. The gun was like new, all right. It showed no rust and seemed to have been only recently oiled. The firing pin was clean, the cylinders heavy with cartridges. But the barrel had been bent sharply when it struck the ground, or glanced off one of the rocks.

"There's been trouble here," Longarm told José, emptying the cartridges into his palm and tossing the gun back into the rocks.

"Trouble, señor?"

"Looks like Opal made her move, tried to get away from Tanner."

"You think he kill her?"

He pointed to the patch of dried blood on the stone. "I think he might have tried—or she might have tried to kill him. It could have gone either way. But I don't see any fresh bodies lyin' around, and the tracks make it pretty clear that two riders left here this morning."

"What we do now?"

"Get a move on. We've already lost too much time."

• • •

Tanner felt a surge of excitement as he followed Opal down the steep slope leading to the canyon mouth ahead of them. She had assured him they were close to Diablo Canyon, and he believed her because he knew how anxious she was to rid herself of him. His wound no longer troubled him as it had. Once he'd gotten her to rip up one of his shirts and bind his ribs with it, he'd been able to ride. It was a good thing the knife had not slipped on through his ribs. Just thinking about that possibility made him wince.

But once he got to that mine, he would repay her. She thought he was unarmed, and knew nothing about the Navy Colt resting in the bottom of his saddlebag. He would bring it out when the proper time came, and then he would have her. First he would make her beg for mercy as he worked her over, and then he would keep working on her until she pleaded with him to take her. He would wait for that before he killed her.

With Opal in the lead, they rode on into the canyon, stopping only to water their horses and fill their canteens in the trickle of a stream that split the canyon. As they pressed on, Tanner noticed drearily that the canyon seemed to twist on forever. By mid-afternoon, however, it widened gradually into a stark, brush-covered flat that shimmered in the sun like the top of a depot stove.

Ahead of him, Opal was riding directly toward a sheer wall of rock. He followed her, wondering irritably what in the hell she was up to—and then saw what he would have missed if they had remained farther out in the canyon: a towering crevice in the wall hidden behind a fold of rock. The giant crack in the wall went as high as the eye could see and seemed to extend for a considerable distance into the rock face. It was, however, only wide enough to admit a single horse and rider.

But Opal did not hesitate. She rode calmly into the crevice and in a few moments had vanished from Tanner's sight. He followed in after her, but he did not like it and called out to her to hold up. Recalling his earlier experiences, he imagined he could hear scorpions scuttling now within the cool rock face only inches from his cheek. Opal slowed some, but not much as they kept going for at least a hundred yards until the crevice widened into an arroyo, which in turn led eventually to another canyon.

It took almost an hour to traverse this canyon until Tanner saw ahead of him an archway of red rock. Beyond this arch, the walls of still another canyon opened before him. Glancing up as he rode under the arch, he saw the arch change its shape until it resembled the head of a scowling devil, horns and all.

Diablo Canyon.

Opal kept on and he followed, studying each side of the canyon for any sign of the mine. Before long he had found it. A great slab of a rock stood beside the mine entrance, keeping it partially hidden in shadow. Unless he had been on the lookout, he might well have ridden past it. Turning his horse, Tanner urged it to a lope and crossed the canyon floor. As he approached the mine entrance, he noted the massive red boulder that sat on a ledge high over the mine shaft, ready at any moment, it seemed, to break loose and thunder down the mountainside.

Tanner knew all about that huge boulder; Jacob Werner had mentioned it often. It was proof positive that Tanner had finally found the lost mine for sure. Riding up to the mine entrance, Tanner dismounted. Opal had followed him, and now turned in her saddle to peer into the mine shaft.

"This here's my mine," he told her. "You hear that?"

"I heard," she told him, smiling contemptuously.

Turning from her, he fairly capered into the mine. Coming from the blazing light of the world outside, he was instantly blinded. He held up, waiting for his eyes to adjust. As he stood there in impenetrable darkness, there came from all sides of him a sudden, paralyzing chorus of rattlers. He had stumbled into a nest of rattlesnakes.

As he turned to bolt back out of the mine, something struck his right boot. Looking down, he saw a rattler hanging onto it, its fangs buried in the toe. Reaching down as he ran, he grabbed the rattler by the tail, yanked it free, then snapped its neck with a quick flick of his wrist. Once out of the mine he flung the dead snake across the canyon. As the snake sailed through the air, his knees turned to water and he began to shake violently. A quick, panicky inspection of his boot revealed that the snake's fangs had not penetrated through the leather.

Taking a deep breath to calm himself, he shook his head in dismay at his stupidity in rushing in there like that without first testing for rattlers.

That cool mine shaft was a perfect place for rattlesnakes to nest; he should have expected it.

He looked over at Opal. As she sat on her horse, he could see the smile on her face. His horror at being surrounded by all those snakes amused her. He walked over to his horse, reached into his saddlebag, and removed the Navy Colt. When she saw it, her hands quickened on the reins, but he grinned and stepped out from behind his horse and leveled the weapon on her.

"Didn't know I had this, did you, bitch?"

She steadied her horse and kept her eyes on him. She wasn't smiling anymore. "No, I didn't, gringo."

"Get down off that horse."

She slipped off her horse and started to walk toward him. "Sure," she said, her dark Apache eyes gleaming.

He wondered if could trust her to stand behind him and hold a torch for him when he reentered the mine shaft. When he went back in to kill the snakes, he wanted to have some help.

"Don't try anything," he told her, "or I'll have to tie you up. And I won't be gentle."

She halted. "No. Don't tie me. But I would like some of that gold."

"So that's it. You don't like bein' poor?"

"Do you, gringo?"

"Hell, no." He studied her for a minute. "All right, I won't tie you up if you'll help me get past them snakes in there."

"I will help you then."

"First, we got to get us a torch so I'll have some light."

"I saw some drywood further back in the canyon."

He holstered his gun. "Get it."

She hesitated only a moment, then turned and hurried down the canyon.

A cold sweat trickling down his back, Tanner advanced cautiously to the mine entrance and peered in. After a while his eyes were able to see pretty far into the mine. He shuddered. All over the cool, hard-packed dirt floor piles of rattlesnakes were restlessly coiling and uncoiling; it was like someone had emptied over the mine-shaft floor an enormous can of worms. And further in Tanner caught sight of three skeletons, their rib cages filled with sand, their skulls smooth cushions now for the snakes slipping over them.

Like him, it appeared, they had dashed into the mine without thinking. But unlike him, they had not been quick enough in their retreat. One of the skeletons was lying facedown, his fleshless arm outstretched toward the mine entrance, as if he were still waiting for someone to pull him to safety. Tanner pulled back from the entrance.

The prospect of going in there and killing those snakes made him go weak in the knees, but when he thought of the gold waiting for him beyond those writhing bodies, he realized he had no choice.

He turned to Opal. "Hold that torch up higher so I can see better."

She did so and he stepped cautiously into the mine shaft, Opal right behind him. He had a club in one hand, his Navy Colt in the other. By this time the rattlesnakes had calmed down some, but Opal's blazing, smoking torch aroused them at once and they began writhing, the sound of their rattlers building quickly to a crescendo. Telling Opal to hold the torch higher, he began firing at the snakes, exploding head after head. When at last he ran out of rounds, he began beating the remaining snakes to death with the club he had brought with him.

Only when he was certain there were no more rattlers—in this portion of the shaft anyway—did he move on, Opal keeping close beside him with the torch. As he proceeded along the shaft, he could not help but admire Jacob Werner and his partner, the ones who had worked it. In Leavenworth those last few weeks before the breakout, Jacob had spoken of almost nothing else; and now, grudgingly, Tanner had to admit that the old bastard had not lied. They had shored up the walls and roofing with huge, solid timbers, each of them braced firmly together so that in places he could not have gotten a knife blade between them.

As he had expected, about twenty feet further along the mine shaft, they came to a storeroom blasted out of the wall. Pushing open the door, Tanner stepped cautiously inside, fearful of more snakes. Opal slipped in behind him and he heard two rattlers in the far corner. In the wavering light from Opal's torch, he saw them slowly uncoiling, their rattles going like mad, their forked tongues licking the air. He used his club on both of them, knocking off one head and bashing the other against the wall. He was becoming almost adept at snake assassination, he realized with a shudder.

The storeroom contained all the tools they would need: drills, sledgehammers, picks, and shovels. Along one wall, tipped up neatly, were two high-sided, ore-carrying wheelbarrows. On a table sat four kerosene lanterns, and beside them a long pine packing crate. Tanner opened the crate's lid carefully and saw that it was filled with dynamite, the neat sticks sitting in sawdust that was still dry. He pulled out a stick to examine it. Dynamite, he knew, would attract moisture, but there was no water in this mine that he could see. He hefted the stick cautiously. It felt just about the right weight, and appeared to be as dry as the day it had been stored here. He put the stick carefully back into its bed of sawdust and lowered the pine lid.

By this time the torch Opal was holding was giving off more smoke than light. He told her to set it down and fill one of the lanterns with coal oil and light it. Once she had done this, they left the storeroom and continued on down the shaft. So far everything was as Jacob had told him it would be, which meant the gold could not be far.

At last they came to the end of the mine shaft. A mound of leather packsaddles were piled up against the end of the passage. Rushing up to the pile, he opened one of the *aparejos* with trembling hands and peered in. Close behind him, Opal held the lantern high, and what he saw made his heart pound. Great chunks of gold ore gleamed dully from inside the *aparejo*. In a near delirium of excitement, he clawed open the other *aparejos* and found still more chunks of gold ore; in a few smaller pouches he found gold dust. One of them

130

he snatched and dropped into the side pocket of his jacket.

It was just as old Jacob Werner had told him!

All they had to do now was go back to the storeroom for one of those wheelbarrows, load it up, and trundle the packsaddles out to the canyon. His horse and the horse he'd be taking from Opal would not be able to lug all this gold back to town, sure as hell not through this heat, but what did that matter? The mine shaft was not going anywhere; he could return to it whenever he needed more gold.

Gawdamighty! He had found Ali Baba's cave!

The prospect so dazzled him that for a moment all he could do was gaze down at the pile of leather pouches before him. Then he came to his senses and realized that he had no time to lose.

"Let's go," he told Opal. "We got work to do."

She turned quickly and started back to the shaft entrance. He took one more long look at the gold-filled *aparejos*, then hurried after her. His shoulder brushed against a wooden stick hanging from the shaft's ceiling. It came loose and thumped to the floor at his feet. Momentarily startled, he came to a halt.

Opal stopped also and, holding the lantern, turned to look at him.

He felt something strike his back lightly as it fell past him to the floor of the shaft. And then something landed on his shoulder, hesitated a moment, then scuttled to the back of his neck. The hair on the back of his neck prickling, he brushed whatever it was off his neck and glanced up to see a wooden cheese box that had been nailed upside

131

down to a cross-beam. From it a dark mass of tarantulas was swarming. In brushing against that lever, he had dumped a nest of tarantulas onto himself!

He heard Opal cry out in horror as she saw two large spiders, then a third plunge directly toward his upturned face. He screamed and thrashed his arms wildly as still more of the furry little bastards rained down upon his head and shoulders. One of them, as terrified and desperate as himself, scuttled up from under his chin, heading toward his mouth. Brushing it off his chin, he ran down the shaft after Opal, who was now far ahead of him. She had dropped her lantern as she ran and her figure blocked out the dim pinprick of light that marked the shaft's entrance.

As he ran, he beat wildly at his jacket and pants, screaming all the while. Near the entrance, he flung off his hat, the brim of which had grown heavy with scuttling tarantulas. As desperate as Tanner, it seemed, two of them raced down his neck and into his shirtfront. He ripped his shirt off. At the same time he felt two more trapped between his back and underwear.

He was still screaming when he dove out of the mine shaft, peeling off his underwear and pants and gunbelt. One tarantula was clinging to his thigh, another to the small of his back, and then another to his right forearm. He flung them off him, shuddering with revulsion.

When at last he stopped thrashing about on the ground, he came back to his senses and found himself free of the tarantulas, but stark naked. He looked around then for Opal, and found himself looking into the bore of his Navy Colt. Opal had taken advantage of his preoccupation to snatch up his gunbelt and holster.

He swore, bitterly.

"I just reloaded your gun," she advised him. "So don't try nothin'."

"You had no intention of helping me. You was just waitin' your chance." He obviously felt betrayed.

"That's right."

"What're you goin' to do?"

"I want you to go on back in thees mine, gringo. And stay there."

"You can't make me do that!"

"Sure, I can."

"But I can't go back in there now," he wailed.

Opal smiled and waggled the gun. "This way you die is better than knife, I theenk."

"You bitch!"

"Yes. I am bitch. But now you never lay hand on me again." She waggled the gun at him. "Go on now. Go back in there to your gold."

"You can't keep me in there. You got to sleep sometime. Soon as you do, I'll get out and finish you."

"We'll see, gringo."

He swallowed, unable to believe how quickly things had turned rotten for him. "Listen," he pleaded, taking an entirely different tack, "there's plenty of gold in there for both of us."

"No, gringo. You would kill me first chance you get."

"How can you say such a thing?"

"Is easy. You will kill me to take my horse so you can carry out more gold."

"That's an awful thing to say. We . . . we're partners."

She laughed scornfully and fired at the ground in front of him. As the round ricocheted off the hard-packed ground, Tanner yelped and ducked back.

"Next time I shoot higher," she told him.

Shaking with fear and anger, he pulled his clothes back on, stepped into his boots, and then—trembling as much in fury as in fear—retreated back into the mine shaft. Stepping cautiously along through the darkness, his ears listening for any soft pattering that would indicate tarantulas, he came at last to the storeroom. Once inside, he lit a lamp and lifted off the lid to the packing crate containing the dynamite. Selecting six sticks, he found fuses, and stuck them into the ends of each one. Then, sticking the dynamite sticks in his belt, he left the storeroom and made his way cautiously back to the mine's entrance. Halting just inside it, he built himself a smoke, then walked boldly out into the canyon.

The Apache bitch was on the other side of the canyon, among the rocks where it was cooler, keeping a close watch on the mine's entrance. As soon as he appeared, she mounted up and rode out of the rocks and headed toward him, brandishing her gun boldly, intent on showing him once again who had all the cards.

He pulled one of the sticks of dynamite from his belt, touched the lit end of his cigarette to the fuse, and hurled it at her. She saw the dynamite in the air and swerved her horse. The dynamite exploded, knocking her and the horse to one side. Tanner sent another stick of dynamite at her. It exploded under her horse, this time blowing her and the horse into the air.

He ran toward her then and saw her scramble to her feet and run off across the canyon. He pursued her for a few yards, then held up, lit another stick, and flung it at her. The smoke and dirt raised by this blast enveloped her completely. When it cleared, he saw her crumpled figure lying facedown in the middle of the canyon.

Hurrying to her side, he found she was still alive, a stream of blood trickling from one nostril. He retrieved his Colt, nudged her with a foot, and saw she did not respond. Meanwhile, the dynamite blasts had set off thundering, teeth-rattling echoes that continued to reverberate within the canyon's walls, causing even the ground beneath his feet to shift uneasily.

Hearing a grinding, scraping sound—resembling a kind of moan—Tanner raised his eyes and saw the huge boulder high above the mine shaft crunching slowly off its precarious perch, sending before it a small avalanche of sand and gravel. It seemed to hesitate for a moment, then it slipped forward a few feet, paused, and with a sudden, fierce urgency, plunged down the mountainside, its momentum increasing with each second. Smashing to the canyon floor with an awful crunch, it rolled on across it, and slammed into the sheer wall opposite. When the dust cleared, the boulder had broken into great chunks and was partially buried in the far wall. And behind it the entrance to the mine had completely vanished under a pile of stone and gravel with nothing to indicate that there had ever been a mine shaft in that canyon wall.

For a moment, Tanner felt a choking despair. But only for a moment. He was not licked yet. He'd get more dynamite and blast his way back into that mine. He knew where the mine was now, and no one else did. One thing was for damned sure. The gold was safe where it was, and it would stay right there until he came back for it.

Intending to waste no time, Tanner walked swiftly after his spooked horse.

Chapter 8

Longarm reined in his horse. José did the same. They had both heard a sudden, sharp peal of thunder. But the sky overhead was perfectly clear. And then there came another blast that seemed to make the canyon walls tremble as the echoes reverberated about their heads with terrific impact. And then came a third blast.

"Dynamite," Longarm said to Jose. "Someone's blasting."

"Tanner?"

"Has to be. Blasting for that gold, maybe."

A moment later there came a sudden, ominous rumbling. The sound built until it filled the air, rose to a crescendo, then subsided. The two men looked at each other, then urged their horses on down the canyon. In a moment they heard the sound of approaching hooves.

Longarm turned his mount into the shadows of the nearest wall, Jose following his example. Then he took out his Winchester and cranked a fresh round into the firing chamber. The clatter of hooves grew louder. Abruptly Tanner swept into sight from an adjoining canyon further down, swung his horse, and loped swiftly on down the canyon away from them.

Tanner was alone. Where the hell was Opal? What had the son of a bitch done to her?

Longarm lifted his rifle to track the rapidly receding rider, then lowered it, aware that at this distance it was unlikely a shot from his rifle would do anything more than warn Tanner that Longarm was on his tail. Again he was thinking about Opal. Those dynamite blasts could have come from an inept attempt by Tanner to blast out the gold in that mine; he might have seriously injured Opal in the process. Or worse: Tanner could simply have tired of her and sliced her up, leaving her to die as he had so many others of his victims. In his mind's eye, Longarm saw again that U.S. deputy Tanner had left for him to find.

"Go after him, José."

"What you do?"

"I'll get after you as soon as I can. It's Opal I'm worrying about. He's left her back there somewhere, and I've got to go find out what happened to her."

"*Sí,* I will follow Tanner then."

"Leave plenty of sign for me, the way Opal did for us. And keep back. Don't get too close to that bastard. He's as treacherous as a rattlesnake."

José urged his horse out from under the cliff

wall, and in a moment he had disappeared around a bend in the canyon. The Mexican knew this country and should have little trouble following Tanner, Longarm told himself; the trick was for him to keep far enough back so Tanner did not find out José was close on his tail.

Longarm rode on and, approaching the canyon from which Tanner had just emerged, saw ahead of him an archway of red stone. As he approached, the angle from which he viewed it shifted, and the rock form assumed the shape of a devil's head. He kept on, riding under it, and entered the side canyon.

He rode on for a considerable distance until he reached the site of the dynamite blasts he had heard earlier. He caught the pungent smell of cordite, and the air was still filled with shifting clouds of dust and debris. Pulling his mount to a halt, he saw where half of a canyon wall had apparently collapsed, and from that point, running across the floor of the canyon, he saw a trail of shale, boulders, and gravel, at the end of which sat the shattered remains of an enormous boulder, a portion of its snout buried in the cliff face.

Then he saw Opal.

She was huddled on the canyon floor, close under a distant wall. He tugged his horse around and rode toward her. As he neared her, he saw the trail she had left as she dragged herself across the canyon floor to where she lay now. Reaching her side, he flung himself from his horse and crouched beside her. Blood was trickling from a corner of her mouth, and some was oozing from her right ear as well.

She opened her eyes, but was too dazed to know who he was. He cradled her head in his arms.

"Opal!" he whispered urgently.

Her eyes focused on him then, and she managed a dim smile. "Custees, you come after me?"

"That's right," he told her. "I disobeyed you."

"I knew you would!"

"How bad you hurt? What happened?"

"Never mind. Get Tanner!"

"Dammit, Opal. How badly are you hurt?"

"Those two bullet holes, they are open again, I think. And my chest, it is crushed from the dynamite."

"My God, what happened?"

"I am such a fool. I think I take Tanner's gun and he will not hurt me while I wait for you. But he take dynamite from the box and send them at me. The explosions throw me in the air and now it is hard for me to breathe. There is such bad pain."

Carefully, he let her head rest on the ground, then gently probed her ribs. When she cried out, his suspicions were confirmed. She had serious internal injuries. The dynamite blasts had broken her ribs, and it looked as if the shattered ribs had punctured her lungs.

"It is your ribs," he told her. "They are broken. Let me bind you up and get you out of here."

"I am not hurt bad, I tell you."

"Of course not."

She closed her eyes. "You treat me like child. All right. I think I am hurt bad. Now leave me and go after Tanner."

Before he could respond, he heard hoofbeats.

Glancing down the canyon, he saw four Navajos approaching. They were armed, their rifles resting across the pommels of their saddles. The lead rider was a heavyset Indian with braided hair that reached almost to his waist. He was wearing a torn leather vest, and his flat, swarthy face was protected from the sun by a large bread-loaf sombrero. He reined his horse in a few yards before Longarm and Opal and gazed down at them through cold, black eyes.

"The Apache woman is dead?" he asked.

"No. She is still alive."

The Indian said something to his companions. They relaxed and put up their rifles. Then the big Navajo dismounted and walked over to Longarm. He went down on one knee and examined Opal.

After a moment he stood up. "She breathes well. I do not think she will die."

"Maybe not, but the son of a bitch who did this left her to die. Now who the hell are you?"

"I am Santoro."

"And I'm a lawman—a deputy U.S. marshal out of Denver. I'm after that gringo who left this woman. What are you doing here? What do you know about this?"

"You ask many questions."

"You didn't just happen to show up in this canyon. What's going on here?"

Santoro shrugged. "The one-eyed one, Sam Dillon, and the other gringo come to me. They would not give me ten dollar to take them to this canyon. And they do not respect my woman, so I leave the gringo town and return to my people and I tell them of the gold in the canyon of the devil."

"Do you know what just happened here?"

The big Indian nodded. "We see it."

"Tell *me* then, dammit."

"We watch, wait for them to bring out gold. But there is much trouble. We see gringo come out of mine shaft with thunder sticks and throw them at the Apache woman."

"I don't see any mine."

Santoro pointed to the debris piled up on the canyon wall across from them. "Under those rocks. Where the gringos cannot get it."

"Nor the Navajos."

"Our people will take it when they need it. There is no hurry. We know it is safe inside that wall."

"So does Tanner."

"When he comes back for the gold, we will kill him."

"Even if he gives you that ten dollars you demanded?"

Santoro shook his head. "I am with my people now. No more white man's firewater. No more of his gold. And my woman and son will live without fear of these gringos." He smiled. "It is better for me now. I am part of the Navajo Nation."

"Well, right now, Santoro, I'd appreciate some help with Opal."

The Indian's anthracite eyes studied Opal's still form. Then he looked back at Longarm. "*Sí,* we take her to my village. There we have good Zuni medicine man. He will care for her."

"Let's go then. You lead the way and I'll follow with her."

Santoro's Navajo band farmed and grazed a large, broad-floored desert canyon. Those few of their hogans built along the base of the canyon's walls were constructed of heavy logs and adobe. Most of their hogans, however, were apartments carved out of the side of an enormous cliff face, a pueblo, or town, taken decades before from the pueblo Indians who first settled the region. Where the rock walls or steps in the cliff side had crumbled or given way, they were repaired with adobe.

At the moment Longarm was close to the top of the cliff face waiting to be allowed into the Zuni medicine man's hogan where Opal was being treated. He was sitting on a bright blanket he had thrown over a boulder, gazing down upon a jumbled, uneven pattern of rooftops and ladders. Far below him, on the floor of the canyon, extensive irrigated fields followed the canyon floor's winding, uneven contours; further on, flocks of sheep drifted over the rolling desert hills abutting the canyon walls.

The Zuni Indian appeared in his doorway and beckoned to Longarm, then stepped aside as Longarm moved past him into the hogan. Longarm found Opal awake on her cot.

"I'm pulling out now," he told her, "going after Tanner."

She brightened. "Good!"

"How you feeling?"

"I am fine, Custees. These broken ribs, they are nothing."

"Don't forget them two bullet wounds."

"The Zuni has take care of them. They are closed now. I feel no more pain."

"That's fine, and once those broken ribs mend, you'll be as good as new."

"I am good as new now. The Zuni has bound my ribs tightly. If you leave now, I go with you."

"Don't talk foolish."

"But you will need my help to track Tanner."

"I sent José to tail him."

"José!" she spat contemptuously. "What good is such a man? This Tanner is an animal. José is no match for such a one."

"He won't be going up against him. Not alone anyway. All he's doing is staying on his tail, leaving a trail for me to follow."

"In this thing José is useless. I know the man. He is a rabbit, Custees. This I tell you for sure. If you not take me with you, I think your heart is too soft."

"Easy now," he said, laughing at her ferocity. "Easy. I'll get the bastard."

"Custis, I am better now," she insisted. "Together we go after Tanner!"

"Be reasonable, Opal. You can't ride with three busted ribs. They'll chew up your lungs. You're better off here."

"You are fool!" she seethed.

Laughing, he bent forward and kissed her on the lips. She did not return his kiss, and when he pulled back she looked away from him. He watched her for a while to see if she would relent. When she kept her eyes averted, he shrugged and left the hogan.

Outside, the old Zuni medicine man was sitting cross-legged on a blanket, smoking his pipe and gazing out over the canyon. His small, nut-brown face was a spiderweb of wrinkles; his white hair, light and feathery, tugged in the hot wind sweeping across the canyon. He understood not a word of English. But when Opal had begun speaking to him in Spanish, he had replied fluently.

Longarm stopped beside him. The Zuni took the pipe out of his mouth and glanced up at him.

"Will she be all right?" Longarm asked.

The Zuni understood the question if not Longarm's words. He nodded at once, his confidence genuine.

Relieved, Longarm turned back to the hogan. "Good-bye, Opal," he called.

She was still too angry to reply. Longarm nodded his thanks to the Zuni and headed for the ladder, the first of many leading to the valley floor and his waiting horse.

José was in a sweat. He had lost track of Tanner, only to come upon him by chance as Tanner rode through a canyon that ran parallel to the ridge José had been following. Tanner was going in the other direction, and if the clatter of his horse's hooves had not echoed so loudly, José would never have known where Tanner was. There was a good chance Tanner was lost; otherwise, he would not be going in the direction he was now taking.

The only way down into the canyon without following the route Tanner must have taken was to cut straight down into the canyon on foot. Such a precipitous descent was not a pleasant prospect, but José could see no other way and he didn't dare lose Tanner again. Señor Long had placed great trust in him, and José did not wish to disappoint the lawman.

As José watched, Tanner disappeared around a bend.

It was late in the day. Tanner would camp soon. If José kept going on foot until he reached Tanner's campsite, he'd have the man. There was no longer any sense in just trailing him; that had already proven impossible for José. So he would capture Tanner and bring him in himself. Perhaps he would make Tanner walk while he, José Santiago, rode behind him. And when Señor Long arrived in Red Rock, José would be waiting with Tanner as his prisoner!

Such an accomplishment, José knew, would amaze his enemies and surprise his friends. In addition, it would make him much more respected. Since his sister's death, he had lost face. This heroic deed would most certainly restore it; and before long, his fame would enable him to marry the lovely Roselita.

Dismounting, he tethered his horse to a scrub pine, and headed for a draw further down that seemed to offer a descent to the canyon floor. Leaning well back to keep himself from losing his balance, he slipped and slid down into the draw until it widened into a ragged fissure, a sharp gap knifing through the layered red rocks that reached all the way to the shadowed canyon floor below. Soon, he was jumping from ledge to ledge as he persisted in his descent.

Abruptly, the draw spilled out onto a broad ledge that thrust out into the canyon like the prow of a ship. Kneeling on the far edge of it, José peered over and saw below him a shallow pool fed by the stream that cut through the canyon. Sizable boulders and slabs of rust-colored rock had broken off the canyon wall and tumbled into the pool.

José estimated that the drop from the ledge to the pool was better than sixty feet. Too far. José retreated from the tip of the ledge and walked back along it until he came upon a crack in the canyon wall that appeared to offer a way down into the canyon. It was as broad as a roadway, and José followed it gratefully until he was confronted by a fissure at least six feet in width that extended across his path. In order to keep on, he would have to leap over it. He backed up, ran to the edge, and leaped. If his feet had not slipped on the gravel, he would have made it easily.

As it was, he fell short and was just able to catch himself with his forearms, cracking them smartly as he did so. He hauled himself up onto the other side of the fissure and kept going. Not long after, he found himself on a narrow ledge thrusting out over an arroyo leading into the canyon. The drop was much less than it would have been from the ledge above, but it was at least fifteen feet, and the ground below was still pocked with broken slabs of rust-colored rock.

But José had no choice. He lowered himself cautiously over the ledge, swung for a moment— trying to pick out a safe spot to land—then let go. He came down hard, his flailing feet striking the wall of the arroyo first, then crunching down onto a gravelly mixture of stone and loose soil at its base. He sank in up to his ankles, and when he pulled himself free, he found his shin was bleeding where he had struck the wall.

He left the arroyo and walked out into the canyon. The tracks left by Tanner's horse were deep and fresh. He would have no trouble following them. Checking his six-gun's load, José started on down the canyon after Tanner.

Once the sun went down, darkness came swiftly in the canyon, but José kept on, grateful for the deep sand along the canyon walls that kept his footsteps silent. After about an hour, José began to smell a camp fire. He kept on. He saw smoke coming from beyond a bend in the canyon.

He had reached Tanner's camp.

That his plan was working sobered him. He promptly held up and ducked behind a boulder to consider his next step. Up until now he had not thought through clearly precisely what he would do when he reached Tanner's campsite. Doubt assailed José, and he found himself wondering if it might not be best after all to go back to his horse and wait for Señor Long to join him, since José had left an abundance of markers for him to follow.

Or perhaps José should just leave Tanner, abandon him to this cruel land, let him become food for the buzzards. It was clear to José that the crazed gringo was lost, and the way he was treating his horse, soon enough he would be afoot. That would finish him as fast as any bullet.

José took a deep breath and chided himself. His

courage was slipping. This was why he was thinking of returning to his horse. What was it Señor Long had told him? It was not necessary to be without fear; all that mattered was to act in spite of the fear. Yes, that was the trick. He would act despite his fear.

He left the boulder and crept forward. When he reached a bend in the canyon, he peered around it and saw Tanner sitting before his fire, his hat pulled down over his face. The man appeared to be dozing. The pungent odor of fresh coffee made José's mouth water and he realized then just how hungry he was.

He drew his six-gun, checked the load, then cocked it. Taking a deep breath, he crept out from the canyon wall. Slowly, cautiously he covered the distance between the canyon wall and Tanner's campsite, his eyes never leaving the figure sitting on the log before the fire. Tanner's stillness made it apparent he had dropped off, encouraging Jose.

A sleeping man might surely be taken without trouble.

At last he was close behind Tanner. Bracing himself, he thrust the barrel of his gun into the small of Tanner's back.

"I have you, gringo!" he cried. "You are my prisoner!"

To José's astonishment, the force of his thrusting six-gun sent Tanner forward facedown into the fire, his hat rolling off his head and on into the darkness outside the ring of light.

He had not captured Tanner, but a dummy instead!

From behind José came a deep, mean chuckle.

He whirled. The gun in Tanner's hand thundered and the slug tore into José's gun, tearing it out of his hand.

"Ain't that pretty fair shootin'?" Tanner remarked.

As José massaged his bleeding right hand, Tanner snatched up José's gun and thrust it into his belt. Then he smiled coldly at José.

"Been waitin' for you. What kept you?"

"Waitin' for me?"

"Sure. I knew you was tailin' me. I figured you'd be catching up soon enough."

José realized that Tanner had no idea he was working with Señor Long, the deputy U.S. marshal who was after him.

Tanner stepped nearer to José and peered at him intently. "Hey, don't I know you? Ain't I seen you in Red Rock?"

"Sure. Maybe you see me in Gold Nugget."

"Yeah. That's the place, all right. What're you doin' tailin' me?"

José shrugged. "I hear you have much gold, so I come after it."

"That's what I figured. Well, you ain't heard wrong. There's gold enough in this goddamn pile of rocks—if I can find my way out of here. That's why I didn't plant a hole in your back. I figure maybe you could help me."

"If I do that," José asked craftily, "will you share the gold with me?"

Tanner laughed contemptuously. "I won't share nothin' with you, greaser. A minute ago you came on me from behind with a cocked revolver. You help me out of this pile of rocks, I might let you live, but I ain't making no promises. Where's your horse?"

"It run off."

"Some horseman you are. You sure you can get us out of here?"

José nodded.

"Okay, greaser. Remember I got your gun. Go on over there across the canyon and find a place to spend the night. Get some sleep. And remember. I sleep light. You try to cut out or cross over to this side of the canyon, I'll kill you."

José crossed to the far side of the canyon, found a grassy spot, and lay down, his eyes on the stars overhead. He had no intention of sleeping; he would stay awake and surprise the gringo when he fell asleep. But José was too exhausted to stay awake, and in a few minutes he had dropped off into a deep sleep.

The aroma of fresh coffee awakened him. He got up, stretched, relieved himself against the canyon wall, then walked across the canyon floor to the gringo's camp fire.

"That coffee," he said, "she smell good."

"Damn right it does," Tanner responded.

But he did not offer José any of it as he broke camp and mounted up. Astride his horse, he looked coldly down at José.

"Well? Get a move on."

"But I do not have a horse."

"I know that, greaser. You got here afoot, so you can lead me out of here the same way. Let's go. I wanta be in Red Rock by nightfall."

Thoroughly dispirited, José looked around for

landmarks, then addressed Tanner sullenly. "You mus' go back the way you came."

"Okay. Just keep ahead of me, and remember I got this here gun trained on your back."

"It will be a long way for me to walk."

"Maybe we'll find your hoss on the way."

José began to trudge ahead of Tanner, his stomach as empty as a rainbarrel in August.

By mid-afternoon, just emerging from the sheer walls of a broad canyon, José came to a stop. "I need water," he told Tanner, "and something to eat."

"Which way's Red Rock?"

"Bear to your right. It is ahead of us, in the valley beyond the plateau."

"Yeah. That's right. I remember now." As he spoke, Tanner drew his revolver and thumb-cocked it.

Startled, José took a quick step back.

"What you going to do?"

"I don't need you no more, greaser."

"But why you do this?" José pleaded. "I have just show you a way out of this badland like you want."

"It ain't nothin' personal. I just don't think its wise for me to let any greaser live who sneaks up behind me with a loaded gun. It might get around."

José turned and bolted back into the canyon. Delighted with this new game, Tanner booted his horse after the fleeing man, firing carefully so that each round kicked up dirt just ahead of his feet, urging him on until his path was blocked by a sheer rock wall. José ran along it, searching for a handhold, anything that would enable him to scramble higher, then flung himself around as Tanner rode closer.

Terrified, José sank to his knees in the sand. "Please," he wailed. "Do not kill me. I will help you."

"You already helped. You showed me the way out of here."

"I will help you even more."

Tanner had been about to send a round into the man's chest. He lowered his gun. "What you gettin' at, greaser?"

"There is a lawman after you. Is this not so, señor?"

Tanner frowned. "Yeah, you're right. How'd you know that?"

"And is his name not Señor Long?"

"That's the son of a bitch, all right. Calls himself Longarm."

"Then I tell you now. He is the one who send me after you. I follow you, and leave trail like the Apache woman so he can find you."

"Well, now. Ain't that interesting."

"Maybe now I tell you how to get him."

"How to get Longarm?"

José nodded eagerly.

"Go on. I'm listenin'."

"We wait here for him to show. When he come toward me, you can kill him."

"You tellin' me since this morning you been leaving signs for him to follow?"

"Yes," José lied. "Soon, I think, Señor Long will be here."

Tanner shook his head contemptuously.

153

"You're full of horseshit, greaser. I been watchin' you, and the only sign you been leavin' behind is piss and shit—and not much of that."

As he pleaded with Tanner, José had been working his way closer to his horse. When he heard Tanner's response, he grabbed the mount's bridle and twisted the horse's head sharply around. The horse rose up on its hind legs and tried to break away from José's grip. José twisted more sharply and the horse stepped sideways and almost went down, rearing frantically, pulling free at last from José's grasp. But he had already spilled Tanner out of his saddle.

Landing hard, Tanner dropped his revolver. José dove for it, snatched it up. But before he could turn around, Tanner caught him from behind, driving him to the ground and reaching around for the weapon. José fought desperately for the gun, but was no match for Tanner, and after a brief struggle, the revolver was back in Tanner's hands.

Tanner jumped back up onto his feet and leveled the gun on José. "Nice try, greaser. Didn't think you had it in you."

He cocked the gun as José lunged at him, stepped calmly back, and pumped three quick shots into José's chest. José cried out and spun to the canyon floor. As the ground under him grew dark with José's blood, Tanner nudged him over onto his back. All three bullets had found his chest inside a circle not more than four inches in diameter.

Good shooting. Damn good shooting.

He glanced skyward. Buzzards would be circling soon. On the ground, José groaned, twisting slightly. He was still alive, but not for much longer. Frowning, Tanner realized that if the greaser had been telling the truth, Longarm would be coming by soon and would most likely find the greaser's corpse.

Contemplating that eventuality, Tanner chuckled. No sense in wasting the opportunity to upset Longarm a little, fill him with rage. As Tanner well knew, a man filled with that kind of hate had a tendency to lose his head and make mistakes—sometimes fatal mistakes.

Tanner took out his big hunting knife and bent over the dying man.

Chapter 9

Longarm came upon José's horse early the next morning tethered to a scrub pine. Puzzled, he dismounted and followed José's boot prints back along the ridge until he saw that José was attempting to reach the canyon below. Realizing that he would not be able to follow unless he also left his horse behind, Longarm returned to his own mount, looped the reins of José's horse about his saddlehorn, mounted up, and continued along the ridge. Less than a mile further on, he found a game trail leading to the canyon floor. Following its narrow, winding course for a good hour, he rode out at last onto the canyon floor. Continuing across the canyon, he found tracks—ominous tracks.

A man on horseback was following close behind another man afoot.

It didn't take Longarm much figuring to guess who the one on horseback might be—and who the poor son of a bitch plodding ahead of him was. Tanner and José, respectively.

Turning his horse about, he followed the tracks, and at mid-morning, after tracing a series of cutbacks through arroyos and draws, and across steep ridges, he came to the mouth of a canyon that led out onto a broad plateau. He quickly recognized a few distant landmarks and knew that if he bore a little to his right and kept on across the plateau ahead of him, he would reach Red Rock.

It was obvious what Tanner had done. He had made José lead him out of this rocky labyrinth, which meant Longarm would most likely find Tanner in Red Rock. He was about to dig his heels into his mount and head out of the canyon when he noticed something out of the corner of his right eye, something odd, out of place. Pulling his hat brim down, he turned to the right and squinted through the glare.

A body was hanging from a gnarled pine growing out of the canyon wall. Dropping the reins to José's horse, he lifted his mount to a run. The closer he got, the more difficult it became for his mind to fight the ugly horror of what his eyes were telling him.

Then he hauled his horse up abruptly and, crying out, turned his head away. It was José all right. Or what was left of him.

Tanner had left another grisly calling card for him to find.

• • •

Finished with his proposition, Tanner leaned back in his chair and gazed around the table at the six men he had assembled, waiting for their reaction. The owner of the Gold Nugget was the first to respond. The fat greaser still held in his hand the damp towel he had been using to wipe off the bar when Tanner invited him to join them at the table.

"Count me out, Tanner," the greaser said, scraping the chair back and standing up. "Maybe you think you know the way back to that canyon, but I am not so sure."

As the Gold Nugget's owner vanished behind the bar, Tanner shrugged and glanced around the table at the others.

"I don't like it," said Fred Boomer, shaking his head unhappily. "That's on Navajo land, ain't it?"

"What the hell's that got to do with it?"

Boomer shrugged. "I just don't like it," he said. "We got a treaty with them redskins, and I sure don't want to be the first one to break it."

"Me neither," said Boomer's companion, Paulie Wagner. "Seems too easy. From what you say, Tanner—all we got to do is ride in there, dynamite the canyon wall, and walk back into the mine shaft and lug away all that gold. Sounds like a fairy tale to me."

"Then you're calling me a liar, Wagner."

"I didn't say that," Wagner insisted.

"I say you're callin' me a liar."

"Hey, now listen, you've got no call to . . ."

And then Wagner saw the gun materialize in Tanner's right hand. He looked from the yawning muzzle to Tanner's cold eyes and got hastily to his feet, his sidekick Boomer getting up also.

"Guess we'll be pushing along," Wagner said.

"My suggestion is you keep on going," Tanner told him.

"Hey, now," Boomer protested, "you ain't got no right to tell us that."

"This here gun in my hand has the right."

Wagner turned to Boomer. "Come on," he said. "Ain't no reason for us to stay in this town anyway."

Tanner smiled. "No hard feelings, boys."

As the two men piled hastily out of the saloon, Tanner looked around at the remaining three men. Leaning back in their chairs, they were grinning at Tanner.

"You sure are handy with that firearm," the tallest one said, his eyes dancing with amusement.

His name was Jud Gilman. He was a tall, raw-boned fellow, all elbows and knees, it seemed, when he'd walked across the saloon to join Tanner earlier. At times, as Tanner addressed him, Tanner got the feeling Gilman was listening to another voice inside himself. The other two were his partners, Ned and Concho. Ned was a fair-haired, freckled youth all chipper eagerness, like a new tail-wagging puppy. Concho got his name from the silver conchas stitched to the hatband of his black Stetson. He was a swarthy man with a long white scar running down his right cheek.

Tanner acknowledged the compliment with a nod.

"Only," Gilman went on, "I don't usually draw my sidearm less'n I intend to use it."

Tanner shrugged and dropped his weapon back into its holster. "Neither do I," he acknowledged.

160

"But I didn't want no gunplay in here. Not while I'm trying to conduct business with you three gents. Well? Are you in?"

Gilman glanced quickly around at his two partners. Each man nodded slightly, their eyes gleaming with suppressed excitement. They liked the sound of all that gold.

Gilman looked back at Tanner. "First I got some questions."

"I'm listenin'."

"How come you need us?"

"What do you mean?"

"If you know where that mine is and you know how to get at the gold, why share it with us? Three perfect strangers."

"I'll need help blowing away the debris in front of the mine shaft. I'll need help lugging the gold out and piling it into the wagon I'll be buying, and desperate men like yourself to guard the wagon while we haul the gold out of that damned place."

Concho smiled, and leaned forward a little, fixing his eyes coldly on Tanner's. "Who you afraid of, mister? And don't give us any more crap, huh?"

Tanner pulled his gaze away from Concho's maniacal, almost hypnotic glare, and saw that Gilman was also smiling.

"What's he drivin' at, Gilman?" Tanner asked.

"We figure you're on the run—something in your manner, so to speak. We can smell that sort of thing, Tanner."

"Can you, now?"

"You goin' to level with us?" Concho asked.

Tanner was not in the least discomfited. He saw

161

no reason at all why he should not tell them about Longarm, and even further, enlist their aid in stopping the son of a bitch. "I had every intention of filling you in on this, gents. I just didn't have the time yet. A lawman's tailing me, name of Custis Long. I just took care of a buddy of his and killed a woman he was sweet on, so I figure he'll come stormin' in here soon enough, and I might need some help."

"Might need some help," said Gilman. "You hear that, Concho? He might need some help with Longarm."

"Damn right he will," said Concho, grinning at Tanner.

"You know this Long?" Tanner asked.

"Yes, we do," said Gilman. "Only we call him Longarm."

"That's the one, all right."

"Never met him personally," Concho said, "but I know some that have. They don't get to see much anymore—not behind walls, that is. This here Longarm is a real hardcase."

"You don't have to tell me. Hell, I just got out of Leavenworth, where that bastard put me."

"So now we got all the cards on the table," Gilman said, "what's gonna be our cut?"

"We split everything four ways."

"Four ways?"

"Sure. I figure that's pretty fair."

"How so?"

Tanner grinned, leaned back in his chair, and tossed down what whiskey remained in his glass. "Because, gents, I'm the only one can take you to that gold."

"Maybe so," Gilman said, "but with Longarm on your back, what're your chances of gettin' that gold out?"

"Not much I'd say," said Ned cheerfully, the young man's sudden entry into the conversation startling Tanner.

Tanner grinned at them. "So keep me healthy then. The four of us should be more than a match for that damned lawman."

"I just wish to hell I could be more sure about that gold," said Concho.

Tanner had expected this and came prepared. He took out the small pouch of gold dust he had rescued from the mine and spilled the glittering sand onto the table.

"Take a look," he said, leaning back. "That's just a sample, I'm telling you. There's plenty more where them came from. Like I explained before, inside the mine shaft there's leather packsaddles filled with gold ore. And its still in there, gents, waiting for us—so much of it, I don't mind cutting it four ways."

It was the young kid's turn to examine the gold dust. As he brushed the gold about the top of the table with his fingers, his eyes gleamed. He glanced up at Tanner. "Hey, there's enough here right now for us to have us a high old time. Maybe we can buy us some women for tonight."

"No," said Tanner, sweeping the gold dust back into the pouch. "I need this here to buy supplies and a wagon—and dynamite."

"There ain't no dynamite in this town," said Gilman.

"There's a mining town south of here," Tanner reminded them.

"Yeah, Yellow Rock. You're right."

"We can buy all we'll need there," Tanner assured him. "Now, gents. Let's have it. Are you in?"

"Four ways?" asked Gilman.

Tanner nodded.

Gilman stared at Tanner for a moment, sizing up the man one last time, then leaned back in his chair and shrugged. "Okay, Tanner. We're in."

Tanner smiled, pleased. "Well now, I think that calls for some fresh liquor."

He beckoned to the Gold Nugget's owner, at the moment serving as barkeep.

"Let's have a fresh bottle over here," Tanner told him.

"Hey, ain't we goin' a little too fast here?" Concho asked. "What about Longarm?"

"With the four of us we don't need to worry about him," Tanner told Concho. "Fact is, it might be a good idea for us to wait right here in town for him. Finish the bastard before we ride out to Yellow Rock."

"Maybe you're right," said Gilman.

The barkeep placed a fresh bottle of whiskey down on the table and returned to the bar. Tanner unstoppered the bottle and poured a round for all of them. They lifted their glasses and tossed down the whiskey, sealing their partnership.

The sun was sending long, slanting shadows across Red Rock's dusty square when Longarm rode in through the late afternoon traffic of wagons, buggies, and horsemen. José's corpse was slung over his horse, wrapped in his slicker, and though José had been dead for at least twenty-four hours, the persistent rocking motion of the horse had disturbed the mutilated body in such a way as to cause dark splotches of blood to discolor the roan's flank. As Longarm pulled up alongside the barbershop, a steady, persistent drip of blood pooled the ground under the horse's belly. Curious onlookers riding by or walking along the sidewalk could not help noticing this grisly fact as they slowed, then pulled up to stare.

Without dismounting, Longarm called in to the barbershop. "Where's the undertaker around here?"

The aproned barber stepped out of his shop, a wet straight razor in his hand, and glanced with some distaste at the corpse draped over the roan's back. Then he peered up through the slanting sunlight at Longarm.

"It's a good thing," he said, "this town don't have no sheriff, or you'd have some explainin' to do, mister."

"I asked if there's an undertaker around."

A crowd was gathering by this time, taking it all in. Wearily, the barber motioned with his straight razor. "Go on around to the back. I'm the undertaker hereabouts. You goin' to pay for the coffin? I'll be usin' good solid pine."

"I'll pay."

The barber's mood lifted somewhat. "I'll be with you soon's I finish with this customer."

Longarm urged his horse on toward the alley leading behind the barbershop, the crowd following after him to the head of the alley, then halting while a few eager onlookers jostled into the front rank to get a better view of Longarm and the slicker-wrapped body draped over the roan.

Longarm was carrying his rifle when he crossed to the Gold Nugget a half hour later. As he entered the place, the saloon silenced and Longarm could feel the stare of every patron in the place. He leaned his rifle against the bar and asked the barkeep for a glass of Maryland rye. Nervously, the barkeep shook his head.

"No Maryland rye, señor."

"I'll take what rye you got then."

"All we got is whiskey and beer."

"Whiskey then."

When it came, Longarm nudged his hat back off his forehead and downed the contents of the glass, slapped it down onto the bar, and pushed it toward the barkeep.

"One more."

"You can have as many as you want, señor. I no count."

"I do."

The barkeep poured. Longarm pulled it close to him, then looked casually about the saloon. The Gold Nugget's patrons were folding their poker games and drifting quietly out of the place.

"What's up?" Longarm asked the barkeep quietly.

"You got trouble, señor."

"For bringing that body in?"

"Ain't you the one rode in here after Jason

Tanner? Ain't you a lawman, the same one killed Sam Dillon?"

"That's me, all right." Longarm tossed down his drink. "And that was the body of José Santiago I just brought in."

"Who did it?"

"Tanner."

The barkeep moistened his lips. It was obvious he had much of importance to tell Longarm, but he was a careful man and needed some urging before he was willing to stick his neck out.

"Let's have it, mister," Longarm told him. "What do you know?"

"It is about this Tanner."

"I'm listening."

"Tanner is back in Red Rock. I am owner of this place. He offer me and some other hombres a chance to go in with him, but I refuse. I listen to what he say so I will know what he is up to. Never would I deal myself into a game with such an hombre. Besides, señor, I hear such talk of gold before, but never do I see any. But three men join him and this afternoon, while they sit here and drink too much, I hear them speak. They say they wait for you to ride in. Then they finish you off and ride to Yellow Rock to buy dynamite."

"Three men you say—and Tanner?"

"Sí, señor. I don' like the look of them three, but Tanner, he is bad enough. I think maybe you better get out of town, señor. And no wait around."

Longarm smiled at the man. "You would appreciate it if I did not cause any trouble inside your saloon."

The owner shrugged, as if to say, "What other course do I have, señor?"

"Where are they now?"

"The hotel, I think. I hear them say they hungry. The only restaurant in town is over there."

Longarm frowned. Funny the four of them hadn't made a move on him before this. He had ridden in with José's body in full daylight and then had spent some time haggling with the barber. As sure as bears shit in the woods, one of the four must've seen him ride in. If not, then surely one or two townsmen, eager to curry favor with the gunslicks, would have hastened to inform them of Longarm's arrival. Maybe the four men had eaten so heartily and drunk so much rotgut they had passed out in their rooms.

Well, whatever the reason, Longarm welcomed the chance to rest up some and gather himself together.

"Go ahead. I know you want to close the saloon," Longarm told the owner. "Just let me rest up in here for a few minutes. I been riding all day through a hot sun."

"Of course, señor."

Longarm finished his drink, took his rifle over to a table facing the batwings, and sat down, the Winchester resting crossways in front of him on the table. Hastily, the owner wiped off the bar, shooed out the three remaining bar girls and the piano player, and with the help of the swamper began setting the chairs up onto the tables.

This accomplished, the saloon owner turned to

Longarm, a pleading look in his eyes. Without hesitation Longarm clapped his hat back on, left the table, and pushed out through the batwings. The sun had gone down by now and the only light came from the cloudless, still-glowing sky. It was too early for stars.

The owner of the Gold Nugget hustled out of the saloon and set a wooden chair down for Longarm. He was careful to locate it away from the more fragile doorway and windows.

"Here, señor," he said. "Sit."

The owner's concern—not for Longarm as much as for the survival of his saloon—amused Longarm, but not wishing to appear ungrateful, he thanked the man and sat down. The owner disappeared back into the darkened saloon and in a minute Longarm heard the rear door slam shut. Longarm checked the loads in his rifle, the .44, and his derringer. Then he leaned back in the chair, his foot braced on a post, the rifle resting across his lap. He had no cheroots left and wished he had. He should have been bone weary, but every sense tingled and he realized he was eager for the upcoming showdown with Tanner and his three hirelings.

The sky grew darker and a few stars appeared in the heavens. By this time all traffic through the square had stopped. No longer were there any buggies, wagons, or horsemen passing the saloon. Further down the square the other saloons had gone silent. Longarm could no longer hear the tinkle of their pianos.

The air was charged; a storm was coming.

Longarm could almost feel the gaze of countless

eyes peering at him from behind windows or from around the corners of buildings. Though the other saloon closest to the Gold Nugget had gone silent, Longarm knew it was probably crammed with eager patrons peering out at him. Longarm felt like a bull waiting to be released into the bullring.

On the other side of the square, a slim figure, gun drawn, stepped out from the alley between the livery stable and the hotel and started to walk toward Longarm. From an alley further down from the Gold Nugget, a shotgun-toting gent with gleaming silver conchas in his hatband stepped into view and began to walk along the wooden boardwalk toward Longarm.

That accounted for two of them; where were the others?

Longarm got to his feet and, carrying his rifle waist high, his finger resting on the trigger, started across the square to meet the first one. Behind this fellow Longarm could see the town's hotel, and he was thinking that maybe that might be where Tanner and the other one were holed up.

And it was Tanner Longarm wanted.

But he had to get past this fellow ahead of him first. As he got close enough to see more clearly the stripling's pale, freckled face and his youthful crop of fair hair poking out from under his hat's sweatband, Longarm felt a momentary qualm. But for his part, the kid apparently felt no hesitation at all as he strode boldly toward Longarm, his six-gun still in his right hand.

Halting abruptly, Longarm called out, "Hold it right there, kid. Take another step and I'll have to use this rifle."

Laughing aloud, the kid lifted his six-gun and fired in one lightning motion. Longarm felt the round slam against the rifle barrel, slamming the weapon out of his hands, the ricocheting bullet snicking through the tail of his frock coat. Dropping to one knee, Longarm drew his double-action Colt and pumped two quick rounds into the kid's chest. The young man appeared to be startled as he gasped and buckled forward to the ground.

Longarm swung around then to see the other one, the fellow with the shotgun, trotting swiftly across the square toward him. Longarm ran past the fallen youngster and ducked into the alley between the hotel and the livery stable, in no mood to stand in the open against a double-barrel shotgun. Swinging around, he flattened himself against the side of the hotel's adobe wall and waited.

Sighting Longarm crouched against the wall, the running figure let go with one barrel. A portion of the adobe wall above Longarm's head disintegrated. Longarm flung himself down flat on the alley floor, sighted carefully, and squeezed off a shot. The fellow with the conchas halted in midstride, as if he'd run into an invisible obstruction. He tried to raise the shotgun. Longarm fired again, more carefully this time. The man sank crookedly to the ground, the shotgun thudding to the ground beside him.

Just above Longarm's head, a second-floor window in the hotel was flung up and Tanner poked his head out. Longarm snapped off his last round at the man, then ran on down into the alley, turned a corner, and entered the hotel from the rear. Crouching in the darkness at the bottom of the stairwell, Longarm reloaded, then started up the narrow steps to the second floor.

Reaching the landing, he found himself in a narrow hallway, four doors on each side. Candles stuck in small alcoves on the adobe walls gave the only light. As Longarm started down the hallway, the second door on his left opened, and Tanner stuck his head out.

He flung a round at Longarm, plowing a gash in the wall behind him. Longarm fired back and took a chunk out of the doorway. Longarm ducked back down the stairs as Tanner sent a determined, but futile fusillade at him, then ducked back into his room and slammed the door shut. In four quick strides Longarm was in front of it. He punched two rounds through the wood paneling, then kicked the door open and charged into the room.

Tanner was alone, crouching down behind the bed as he finished reloading his Colt. Before Longarm could cut him down, he flung the Colt onto the bed and flung up both hands.

"Don't shoot, Longarm. I'm your prisoner."

Longarm caught himself, then lowered his weapon, sorry he hadn't still been shooting when he burst into the room.

"Where's the other one, Tanner?" Longarm asked. "Number four? I heard you found three men foolish enough to throw in with you."

"He's gone. He lit out when he saw what you did to his two buddies."

"Why don't you do the same thing, Tanner? Why don't you light out, make a run for it?"

"Now why should I do a fool thing like that?

You'd just cut me down. It's what you been waitin' to do."

"I'll make a deal with you, Tanner. I'll throw my gun onto the bed alongside yours. I'll let you walk right on past me out of this room. You'll be a free man."

"You must think I'm crazy."

"Look at it this way. Once you get out of this hotel, you'll have a better than even chance of making it out of town alive."

Tanner grinned. "My, my, you sure are anxious to gun me down, ain't you. But I can understand that. You saw what I done to that fool greaser was sidin' you."

"Yes, you bastard. I saw."

Tanner looked for a long moment at Longarm, as if he were considering the lawman's offer to let him walk out. "I want a smoke," he said, reaching for the makings in his vest pocket.

"Don't let your hands move too fast. That's all the excuse I'll be needing."

"Sure," Tanner said.

Tanner quickly, expertly built his cigarette, licked it, then planted it into his mouth. Snapping a match to life with his thumbnail, he lit the cigarette, then slumped back against the wall, drawing the smoke into his lungs, a mean smile on his face.

"I know how you feel," he told Longarm. "You want to kill me so bad, you can taste it."

Longarm said nothing.

"The way I see it," Tanner went on, "you just ain't got the guts to pull that trigger—not in cold blood, anyway."

173

"All right," Longarm said, waggling his six-gun. "We've talked enough. Let's go."

"Hey now, wait a minute. What's your hurry? You just offered to throw your gun onto the bed and let me get past you. You still want to do that?"

Longarm did not want to do that. He was furious at himself for having suggested such a fool thing. On the other hand, he did not want to bring this man in alive.

Longarm watched him warily. "What I want is to see you dead, Tanner."

Tanner shrugged. "All right. I'm game. Drop your gun onto the bedspread and I'll walk out of this room. I got a horse all saddled in the livery. I'll light out and then you can come after me." He grinned then. "And may the best man win."

Longarm tossed his revolver onto the bedspread beside Tanner's. He knew he was doing a fool thing, but the fresh memory of what Tanner had done to José was too much for him. All he wanted was to nail Tanner.

Longarm stepped aside to let Tanner leave the room. As Tanner stepped between Longarm and the bed, a knife flashed in his hand; he struck like a rattler, the blade sinking into Longarm's side. It was only a flesh wound, but the sharp pain and the surprise of the attack were enough to stun Longarm momentarily. Snatching up his Colt off the bed, Tanner smashed Longarm on the top of the head with it. But Longarm had seen the blow coming and managed to fling up his forearm and ward off most of the blow. Groggy nevertheless, he saw Tanner halt at the door, a stick of dynamite in his hand. Touching his lighted cigarette to the

174

fuse, Tanner tossed the stick onto the floor at Longarm's feet, then bolted from the room.

Longarm reached down for the dynamite, but it was still rolling and vanished under the bed, the fuse sputtering. Longarm did not hesitate, he flung open the window behind him, and jumped to the alley floor. It was quite a drop, and he was still on his hands and knees when the blast came. He felt the wall behind him explode outward, large pieces of adobe catching him on the back, crushing him to the ground, the noise of the blast deafening him; he felt as if someone had punched him in the back, and struggling to draw a breath, he crawled out of the alley onto the square.

He was trying to push himself upright and having no luck at all when he heard Opal's warning cry.

"On the livery roof, Custis!" she cried. "Look out!"

Behind him a shotgun blast sounded. Glancing up, Longarm saw Tanner's third recruit—an emaciated rope of a man—topple off the livery stable's roof. The man could not have been more than fifty yards away and he had an unobstructed view of Longarm's sprawled figure. From that distance he could not have missed.

Still unable to get up, Longarm turned his head and saw Opal standing beside the dead man Longarm had finished earlier. It was this fellow's shotgun she had just used to save Longarm's life.

Twice Longarm started to get up onto his feet, but his legs were not functioning. Each time he went down hard. Those chunks of adobe driven by the dynamite blast had severely bruised his legs—or had it been that jump from the hotel window?

He was thinking about making another attempt to get up, and Opal was running toward him, when out of the livery stable galloped Tanner, heading straight for his sprawled body. Fumbling for his derringer, Longarm waited until the last possible moment, then rolled aside. Horse and rider flashed past. Tanner flung a wild shot down at Longarm, then turned his horse around and headed back out of town. Longarm staggered up onto his feet, flung up his derringer, and fired after Tanner. He missed, steadied his arm, and fired again.

A titanic explosion rocked the square as Longarm's bullet must have hit one of Tanner's dynamite sticks.

The blast rocked Longarm backward, but he put his head down and remained doggedly on his feet as Tanner's saddlebags—and maybe bits and pieces of Tanner himself—whistled over his head. Slowly the dust settled and Longarm found himself contemplating a grisly, stained hole in the ground where once there had been a horse and rider.

Longarm turned around then to see Opal running toward him. She had risked her life to ride after him like this, and the kick from that shotgun could have reinjured one or two of her ribs. But she seemed healthy enough as she neared him, her arms outstretched. She was calling out to him, but his ears were ringing so much he could not hear a word she was saying.

But that didn't matter. They'd have plenty of time to talk later.

Chapter 10

United States Marshal Billy Vail watched Opal wistfully. Laden down with beribboned hatboxes, shoe boxes, and dress boxes—all of which she insisted on carrying upstairs herself—she was hurrying from the Windsor Hotel lounge on her way upstairs, so eager was she to unpack and examine today's extravagant purchases. As she crossed the hotel lobby and started up the wide marble stairs, Longarm glimpsed two bellboys hurrying eagerly up the stairs after her, more than anxious to help this lovely lady get to her room.

"You sure you can afford to buy her all them goodies, Longarm?" Vail asked.

"She saved my life, don't forget. Besides I consider it a kind of penance."

"Penance?"

"For being such a horse's ass as to let Tanner

clobber me like that in the first place."

"You wanted him to make a break, didn't you?"

"I didn't want to get blown from here to hell."

Billy chuckled. "However you managed it, he's dead, and I'm grateful and so are quite a few others. But you know," he went on slyly, "you didn't have to bring Opal all the way up here to testify before the board of inquiry. That board would've believed your account of Tanner's death without her testimony."

Longarm grinned. "Just don't you tell *her* that. You'll spoil everything."

Vail laughed.

Longarm lifted the bottle of Maryland rye and filled both their glasses. Then he leaned back, sipped the rye, and looked about him at the Windsor Room's upholstered leather booths, the maroon-and-gold drapes, the old buffalo head on the wall behind the bar. It was good to be back in civilization once more, where a man could purchase what really mattered, like Maryland rye and a fresh pack of cheroots. He had been determined to quit smoking until he walked into the hotel lobby a few minutes ago and saw the slim package of cheroots sitting in the tobacco shop's display case.

Oh, well. He'd quit for good next week.

"About that lost mine," Vail said.

"What about it?"

"You think anyone else knows about it?"

"Sure. Santoro and the rest of the Navajo Nation. Opal said they will clear away the rubble from the mine's entrance, and then take out all the gold they need, use it to help finance the tribe's expenditures, like purebred sheep, farming equipment, looms for their rugs, and maybe some weapons if the white man tries to take back their land despite the treaty."

"They got no worry on that score. No one's going to want to settle in that desert country."

"And that's precisely what the Navajos are counting on."

"So I say let them keep the gold."

"That's big of you."

"That's big of the United States Government." Vail downed his drink and sidled out of the booth. "Guess I'll be packin' it in," he said. "The hour is late and you and Opal got things to do."

"Can't argue with that."

"And since you got all that money, you take care of the tab."

Longarm stepped out of the booth, smiling. "It will be my pleasure."

Opal opened her door on Longarm's second knock. He hurried quickly into the room and closed the door hastily behind him.

"My God, Opal," he said, staring at her. "You should never open a door like that."

"What's the matter? Don't you like how I look?"

"That ain't the point. What about all them lovely dresses and silk panties you bought today?"

"I can try them on later."

She moved into his arms, lifted her lips to his, and kissed him hard, her mouth working sensually. His head swimming slightly, he lifted her

179

naked body in his arms and carried her over to the bed.

She could always show him how her new dresses looked on her later—much later.

Watch for

LONGARM AND THE LONGLEY LEGEND

143rd novel in the bold LONGARM series

from Jove

Coming in November!

WESTERNS!

at least a savings of $3.00 each month below the publishers price. Second, there is never any shipping, handling or other hidden charges—Free home delivery. What's more there is no minimum number of books you must buy, you may return any selection for full credit and you can cancel your subscription at any time. A TRUE VALUE!

Mail the coupon below

To start your subscription and receive 2 FREE WESTERNS, fill out the coupon below and mail it today. We'll send your first shipment which includes 2 FREE BOOKS as soon as we receive it.